CAROLY

Born into the Pertwee dynasty, Carolyn soon displayed family talent for acting and writing. Graduating with honours from RADA, Carolyn joined The Old Vic Company on its world tour and enjoyed her first big break playing opposite Vivien Leigh in *Duel of Angels*. Then followed a successful stint in television appearing in many dramas including *Compact,* a TV soap in which she played a suicidal kleptomaniac.

Carolyn married Coeks Gordon and following the birth of her two daughters turned to writing with a commission from Warner Sisters for her sitcom *Rosie and Dud.*

Numerous plays were written and performed across local and national theatres around London, and BBC Radio Four commissioned Carolyn to write *The Beautiful Couple* for their afternoon play slot, starring Julia McKenzie and Ronald Pickup. Reviews in the national press were glowing.

Her quartet of plays, *Sexologically Speaking*, was a sell out at the O.S.O Arts Centre in 2007. This was followed by *Between Friends,* a tense drama written with Rosalind Adler.

Carolyn wrote the book for the musical *A Bowl of Cherries,* performed at the Charing Cross Theatre in March 2012.

Carolyn is the Deputy Chair of Actors and Writers London, a 175 strong collective that puts on regular rehearsed readings. Still married to Coeks, she lives in Barnes, enjoying her other role as grandmother of four.

Feeling the Fear is Carolyn's first published collection of short stories.

FEELING
the FEAR

And other intriguing tales

FEELING
the FEAR
And other intriguing tales

CAROLYN
PERTWEE

Alliance Publishing Press

Alliance Publishing Press

Published by Alliance Publishing Press Ltd
This paperback edition published 2012
Copyright © 2012 Carolyn Pertwee
The moral right of the author has been asserted
Alliance Publishing Press Ltd

ISBN-13: 978-0-9552661-9-5
Typeset in Times New Roman & Garamond Pro
Book & Cover Design by Mark James James

For Coeks, Dani *and* Tanya

CONTENTS

FEELING *the* FEAR

To go or not to go, that is the question. Linda sat in the airport lavatory clutching her evacuated stomach. She prayed that the twenty milligrams of Diazepam swilled down with vodka would soon give her the courage she required to step outside and catch the plane for a two week holiday in Portugal. She knew she was being silly, she knew she had far more chance of being killed in the mini-cab on the way to Gatwick than in an aeroplane. She was, after all, a rational human being.

Hugh had been so patient and reassuring the night before.

'Feel the fear Lin, tackle it head on. It's the thought that's freaking you out.'

But it wasn't just the thought; she could not eradicate from her mind last night's dream, so vivid and so real. Roaring down the runway, an ear shattering explosion, the plane shaking and rocking violently from side to side, the cabin filling up with smoke, the overhead lockers flying open and thousands of oranges cascading out on top of her, their skins bursting open and bright red blood spurting out, splattering her face and hair. She tried to breathe but a body fell on top of her. She was suffocating as she tried to push the body away.

It was Hugh. She had been dreaming. Hugh took her in his arms and hugged her awake. Linda had sat up in bed, surveying their bedroom with relief till her eyes took in the bulging suitcase on the floor across the room.

She turned to Hugh and said, 'I'm not going tomorrow. I've got too much work on. Anyway I'd much rather spend my 30th birthday with you.'

Hugh smiled at her. 'You've been dreaming about planes again haven't you?'

Linda nodded. She had frequent nightmares about flying but this one had been different, this one felt as though she was foreseeing her own death. She started to tell him the dream but then clammed up as she remembered the old saying, 'Friday night's dream Saturday told, will always come true, however old.' It was just after midnight on Saturday morning.

'Oh God!' she said. 'If I tell you it might come true'.

'Oh Piglet!' Hugh tried not to show his exasperation, he kissed her on the tip of her nose. 'Of course you must go. If you give in to this fear you'll never get on a plane again. You've got to be brave. When you're actually up there it'll be a piece of cake, you'll see, you'll wonder why you were getting in such a state.'

Hugh didn't understand fear; he exuded confidence in everything he did. He wasn't afraid to be himself, holding strong and often controversial views on life which he had no inhibitions in airing both as a journalist and amongst their many friends. Linda idealised him and after five years of marriage still sought his admiration and approval. Hence this holiday with her old, recently divorced school friend Virginia, who had suggested she come over to celebrate her birthday.

Linda had been secretly hoping that Hugh was planning some sort of surprise for the big day and so was doubly disappointed when he insisted that she went.

She looked at her watch, it was five to seven. She should

have gone through the gate by now. The plane was scheduled for take off at seven thirty.

'Come on, girl, stop thinking about it. Just get up and go - piece of cake,' spoke the voice of reason.

Linda obediently got up, flushed the toilet, picked up her hand luggage and stepped outside. She went over to the basins and washed her hands, surveying her face critically in the mirror, her wide set brown eyes looked strangely disconnected as they stared forlornly back.

She looked tired and her make-up had that end of the day look about it. She reapplied some lipstick, cursing the mole above her lip which she detested and everyone else told her was attractive. She still looked like a schoolgirl with her turned up nose, another feature she disliked and had earned her the name of 'Piglet' when she was at school. She combed her straight fair hair cut pageboy style emphasising the squareness of her jaw.

'Take a good look, Lin, you might never see yourself again, you're going against your horoscope - remember?' the inner voice whispered in her ear.

Please don't let's go through that again. Linda closed her eyes and tried to forget but its stark message wouldn't go away:

'Use today to reflect, make no rash decisions and do not undertake a journey - stay at home and attend to matters of the heart...' She'd shown it to Hugh at breakfast suggesting that she change her flight to later in the week or perhaps not go at all.

'Don't be absurd Lin! Do you realise if everyone believed that garbage one twelfth of the world's population couldn't go to work!'

Of course he was right, she was just using the horoscope to justify not getting on the plane. She must pull herself together, stiff upper lip and all that. She breathed deeply drawing her shoulders back and set off purposefully out of the Ladies toilet.

'This is the final call for passengers flying to Faro on Flight number 202, will they please go immediately to gate thirteen.' Linda's ears pricked up at the announcement and her heart began to thump as she headed for gate thirteen.

'You know, Lin,' the inner voice spoke again, 'you don't have to go, you can turn back now and go home, nobody's stopping you. Yes, Hugh will be cross, and yes, Virginia will be disappointed - but just think what you might be avoiding.'

Linda stopped. She was just a few feet from the gate, the choice was still hers, she was still in charge of her own destiny.

'Don't be a bloody idiot,' came the other voice. 'Nothing is going to happen to you except in two hours time you'll be in Portugal and you'll wonder what on earth you were doing standing dithering at Gatwick for - right?'

A few minutes later she was walking down the enclosed gang-plank to the plane's entrance like a lamb to the slaughter.

She felt unreal as she fastened her seat belt for the fifth time bouncing forward to ensure it was secured. They had been waiting for twenty minutes while a mechanic in an orange boiler suit was opening and closing a fire exit door a few rows in front of them. The plane was packed but the conversation muted. Linda was in an aisle seat next to a plump and busy woman sorting out the contents of a bulging bag. She kept smiling at Linda who smiled briefly back and looked away. She couldn't talk; her fear needed her undivided concentration.

The mechanic opened and closed the door yet again and then scratched his head.

'What do you think he's doing with that door?' said the busy woman. 'It's making me nervous.'

Before Linda could reply the captain burst out of the cockpit and joined the mechanic.

'What's going on?' he barked. The captain was an unhealthy looking man with a pale grey pallor: his uniform jacket had one button missing and fitted uneasily round his short stocky frame. He stood straight-legged, his arms folded, his head jutting forward as he listened to what the mechanic, who spoke quietly out of earshot, had to say. Both men then inspected the door. The captain straightened up and said quite clearly, 'Oh, come on - it's all right.' With that he turned and strutted back into the cockpit, slamming the door behind him. The mechanic shrugged, picked up his tool bag and walked away down the aisle.

Linda felt paralysed with fear, if she could have moved her limbs she would have insisted on getting off the plane. The engines had started to warm up and the air hostesses had stepped into place to demonstrate, in the unlikely event of an accident, the various safety measures. She tried to concentrate on what they were saying and rationalised with herself that they wouldn't be doing this job if they seriously felt they were at any moment about to die. The plane started to taxi towards the runway. Captain Cox announced himself and their imminent departure. Linda picked up her book and looked at it grimly.

'Excuse me,' the busy woman said.

Linda pretended not to hear and stared intently at the page as though engrossed. She then felt her sleeve being tugged.

She turned towards the woman, 'Yes?'

'You've got your book upside down.' She smiled sweetly and with great understanding. 'I'm Mary by the way.'

The noise of the engines obliterated any further conversation. Linda breathed in and out deeply trying to control her mounting panic. The plane hovered a second revving and straining at the leash before it started off along the runway gathering speed by the second. Linda could scarcely breath now, she was feeling the fear - Oh God was she feeling the fear!

In a minute it'll go up and then the worst will be over, Linda told herself. The plane was still on the ground at full speed - there can't be much more runway left!

Mary suddenly clutched Linda's arm, her face was stricken. 'This should have gone up by...' she didn't finish her sentence.

There was a deafening roar and then a grinding noise as the engines were thrown into reverse and the body of the plane shook violently. Linda turned round to seek reassurance from the other passengers but their faces were white masks of terror. The plane was trying to stop but Linda knew it was too late and she could almost feel the heat from the flames that at any moment would engulf them; each particle of hair on her head felt as though it were being pulled out from the roots, her heart was beating and banging against the wall of her chest. She gasped for air, Mary grabbed her hand, they squeezed each other hard and then brought their heads together. She thought of Hugh safe at home. She thought of her recently widowed mother now about to lose her only daughter. She saw them both standing side by side staring at her coffin – and then the plane miraculously stopped.

The deathly hush suddenly evaporated and everyone began to speak at once anxious to share the feelings that all of them had just experienced and the joy of being alive.

The terse voice of Captain Cox came through: "Owing to a technical fault we have decided to abort take-off. Please remain calm and leave your seat belts fastened."

Twenty minutes later the passengers of flight number 202

returned on spongy legs to a hospitality lounge at Gatwick to await the repair of the technical fault. Linda and Mary had supported each other off the plane and were sitting side by side on a comfortable sofa drinking champagne - the compliments of Vulcan Airways.

'This is a bribe if you ask me,' said Mary downing her champagne with gusto. 'And I'm going to need a few more to get me back on that awful plane!'

'Nothing will get me back - I'm going home,' Linda said.

Mary's jaw dropped open. 'You're not!' she gasped. 'Gosh you are brave!'

'Brave? Hardly - my husband's going to be furious with me.'

'I'd love to have the courage to walk away but I feel like I've been sort of programmed to go - if you know what I mean,' she laughed nervously. 'Besides my daughter's expecting me, I can't let her down now can I?' She looked appealingly at Linda.

'No, of course you can't.' Linda leant forward and kissed Mary on the cheek. She smelt of sweet powder and lily of the valley scent. The two women swiftly bade each other farewell.

Linda felt like a Judas as she walked away from Mary. Perhaps she should have told her about the horoscope and her dream. She turned round at the door and looked back across the room; Mary was once more immersed in rummaging through the contents of her bag. She sent this kind woman a silent prayer before she left the room.

An hour later Linda sunk blissfully into her seat on the train back to Victoria. She had decided not to telephone Hugh in case he'd tried to persuade her to get back on the plane. Much better to just turn up, she assured herself, 'fait accompli'. Fortunately she wasn't being met at Faro airport. Hugh had booked her into a hotel for the night. She would ring Virginia and explain everything when she got home. Vulcan Airways had been very civil when she told them that the false take-off had brought on an asthma attack; she'd wheezed several times before embarking on the conversation. They offered her a full refund and had her luggage removed from the faulty plane. Now all she had to face was Hugh.

The taxi dropped Linda off outside the pretty little mews house in Pimlico at quarter to eleven. She was surprised to see that the downstairs lights were off; Hugh usually worked late into the night. Tobias their tabby cat was sitting on the doorstep looking vexed.

Linda bent down to stroke him. 'Has that naughty Hughie locked you out?' She opened the front door. Tobias swept the length of his body against her legs before slithering through in front of her. Linda closed the door and leaned against it savouring the moment of once more being in the home she thought she'd never see again. She walked into the sitting room switching on the light. There was an empty bottle and a half filled glass of red wine standing on the coffee table. She smiled to herself. Hugh rarely drank and red wine made him horny. She began to undress watched indifferently by Tobias who had arranged himself along the back of the sofa. She stripped naked then slipped out into the hall and listened – all was quiet. She tiptoed into the downstairs bathroom and quickly showered the strains of the day away.

Five minutes later, refreshed and clad only in a T-shirt which barely covered the edge of her bottom, she crept up the stairs to face her husband.

The door to their bedroom was slightly ajar, a Bach fugue,

Hugh's favourite, was playing on the radio. Linda realised she was trembling, she felt like a child about to encounter the Headmaster for misbehaving. Hugh was fifteen years her senior and could be very stern. She edged the door open. The room was lit by a warm glow from the bedside lamp. She leant sideways and peered in. She blinked and looked again; it wasn't Hugh sitting up in bed but a statuesque woman, naked from the waist up: her splendid breasts brazenly displayed like two prize melons above the sheets. She was reading *A Brief History of Time* by Stephen Hawking and sipping a glass of red wine. Linda recognised her at once; it was Delia Plume, the witty editor of *Thinking Woman*. She had become something of a cult figure, known for her acidic pen and caustic wit and, in recent years, had livened up many a late night chat show on T.V. Hugh wasn't in the room but the en-suite bathroom door was closed, his striped towelling dressing-gown was strewn across the bed, his clothes lay abandoned on a chair.

Linda retreated behind the door again, her heart once more on the rampage. Suddenly everything fell into place: Hugh's insistence on her going away, his distracted air, the way he'd hastily put down the phone when she'd walked into his study the previous day, the lack of love making over the past few months, but he'd been working round the clock and she had accepted his excuses of being too tired. Even that very morning he'd slipped early out of bed before she'd woken; in the past they'd always made love before a separation. Everyone had warned her before she married Hugh that he was a womaniser, even her vague and scatty mother, who was a mine of mis-quotations, had said 'You'll have to watch him, Lin, a tiger doesn't change his stripes or do I mean zebra, dear?'

But Hugh had promised that his days of womanising were

over, that he took his marriage vows seriously and like a fool she had believed him. She felt intimidated by the impostor in her bed - not only her superior breasts - Hugh laughingly referred to hers as 'mini mams' but by her obvious intellect as well; Linda had never got past the first chapter of Stephen Hawkings' book; nor would she want to before having sex and with someone else's husband! Suddenly flight 202 to Faro seemed an idyllic dream with Mary cosy and comfortable at her side. Instead she was standing in a nightmare scenario facing a confrontation with her husband and his intellectual mistress which would effectively end their, what she had thought, happy marriage.

'You can walk away,' said the inner voice. 'Nobody knows you're here...'

'But I shall always know and I couldn't live with that,' Linda silently replied. She pushed open the bedroom door and boldly stepped inside.

Delia looked up startled, her arm jerked out sideways, the red wine tossed violently in the glass like a sudden tidal wave. 'Christ almighty, who are you?' her voice conjured up smoke filled bars. She was a magnificent looking woman on a grand scale: her faded ginger hair piled high on her head in a cluster of careless curls, heavy lidded olive eyes flecked with amber, her face a mass of freckles.

'You know perfectly well who I am.' Linda glanced over nervously to the still closed bathroom door.

'Do I?' Delia looked her up and down and raised an eyebrow; Linda wished she had left her clothes on. 'Hugh told me there was a *cat* - he certainly didn't mention *you!*' She half smiled showing the famous gap between her two front teeth.

Linda was so taken aback by this woman's apparent lack of shame or modesty, not even bothering to cover up her breasts, that she couldn't think of how to continue the conversation. She tugged her T-shirt down and with as much dignity as she could muster walked across the room towards the bathroom. She stopped and turned towards Delia who was watching her curiously.

'You've got five minutes to get out of my house - I'm going to speak to Hugh,' Linda indicated the bathroom door.

'*Your* house?' Delia said incredulously.

'Yes, *my* house,' Linda felt her strength returning. 'I'm Hugh's wife.'

Delia looked aghast, she put her glass down. "His *wife*? Oh my God!' she said and covered her head with her hands. 'What a mess! You're supposed to be in Portugal.'

'Yes, well I'm not – sorry to have been so inconsiderate.' Linda replied sarcastically, feeling the balance of power returning in her favour. 'Now will you please *go!*'

'What a cock-up!' Delia said, ignoring Linda's last remark.

'In the circumstances - not an expression I would use!' Linda quipped back. 'And now, if you don't mind, I'm going to speak to my husband.' She opened the bathroom door; it was hot and steamy and smelt of Badedas, a towel lay crumpled on the floor but Hugh was not in sight.

She stepped back into the bedroom. 'Where is he?' She suppressed an urge to peer under the bed; French farce was not Hugh's style.

Delia lowered her hands and looked at her watch. 'He's on his way to Portugal,' she said wearily. 'To surprise you on your birthday.'

Linda stood colt-like staring at Delia in disbelief and then burst into tears. Delia clambered out of the bed, pulling on Hugh's dressing gown. She hurried over and put her arm round

Linda's shoulders; the dressing gown felt damp and smelt of Hugh. She led her back to the bed where she sat her down and listened sympathetically while Linda recounted the day's events. She didn't even laugh when Linda told her about the horoscope and said that wild horses wouldn't have got her on that plane either. She then explained to Linda that her flat was being treated for dry rot and that Hugh had offered her the use of the house for a few days while he was in Portugal in return for feeding the cat.

'Now,' she said, 'we've got to get you off to Portugal, with any luck we might get you on the same plane as Hugh. I don't think his was leaving till one o'clock.'

Thirty-five minutes later at 11.40 p.m. the two women were bowling along the M4 towards Heathrow Airport in Delia's red Fiat car. She drove in the slow lane just in case any speed cops were around; she was over the limit, though, she assured Linda, one of her ex-husbands said she drove better when she was fuelled with drink.

Linda had been amazed at the way Delia had taken over; it seemed she had contacts in all the right places including British Airways with whom she'd organised the ticket on condition it was collected as near to midnight as was possible. It was the same flight as Hugh's though he was unaware that she was joining him.

'You can surprise the old sod instead – people who organise surprise parties should be shot!' Delia scoffed. She was surprisingly derogative in all her references to Hugh, but then she'd known him for years she said. They'd cut their teeth together on the Guardian as journalists.

'We were younger than you,' she snorted derisively, 'if that's possible.'

Linda laughed. 'Oh come on Delia! I'm not that young.' She looked at her watch. 'In fact, in exactly 10 minutes I shall be 30. I was born on the stroke of midnight.'

Delia grinned. 'It's my birthday next week – I wish I was going to be 30.'

Linda looked warmly across at her as they drove along; she felt that they were kindred spirits and wondered why Hugh had never introduced them and they shared the same birth sign.

Suddenly the Fiat was flooded with a harsh light as a large lorry pulled up close behind them.

Linda turned round to look, 'Oh gosh! He's a bit close for comfort!'

'Certainly is. I'm pulling out.' Delia pulled sharply out into the middle lane not noticing the white van coming up close behind them causing the driver to swerve into the third lane, blasting his horn and gesticulating at them furiously. 'I detest white vans,' said Delia unreasonably, 'they always drive too fast.'

At that moment the lorry they had avoided pulled up alongside them and overtook them also blasting his horn.

'Bastard!' Delia yelled. She noticed the Spanish number plate, 'A Spanish Dick on wheels! We'll show him!' She put her foot down on the accelerator.

'Please don't,' said Linda, her heart was racing.

Delia glanced at the frightened face beside her. She patted Linda on her arm and reluctantly pulled into the slow lane allowing the lorry to get away. 'Sorry love,' she said. 'You've had enough scares for one day.'

An exit sign for Terminals 1, 2 and 3 appeared.

A thousand miles away Flight 202 had landed safely at

Faro Airport. As Mary stepped out of the plane the heat of an exhausted day wafted up to meet her. She looked up into the ink blue sky alive with winking blinking stars and let out a long sigh of relief. She thought about her frightened little friend with whom she'd thought she was going to die and felt sad that she didn't know her name.

The Fiat turned off the motorway. Linda checked the time and smiled, they would make it just in the nick of time. She felt happier than she'd ever felt in her life; her fear of flying had somehow magically disappeared. She turned to Delia, 'I don't know how to thank you, you've just been wonderful.'

'You can thank me by staying on that plane and not reappearing half way through the night and scaring me half to death!' They both laughed.

'No way!' Linda said, 'and I shall be with Hugh. I'll give him your love, shall I?'

Delia looked across at Linda, their eyes met briefly.

'Yes, give the old bastard a kiss from me. Tell him he's a lucky man.' She brought her eyes back to the road too late to avoid the Spanish lorry slewed across their path, the white van in flames, crushed beneath it. The back doors of the lorry had swung open, wooden crates were toppling and tumbling out smashing on to the ground and breaking open. Thousands of oranges spilled out on to the road.

The Fiat and its passengers didn't stand a chance.

It was one minute to twelve.

Hugh never knew what happened on that night in June. He could only speculate on why his wife and mistress were killed in the same car on the way to Heathrow Airport and it would haunt him till his dying day.

RUBY *from the* EMERALD ISLE

September 30ᵗʰ 1997

The ringing pierced the silence of the night, sharp and insistent. Kitty Trotter sat bolt upright in bed and slammed her hand down on her innocent alarm clock with such force that it skidded sideways and landed on the floor. The ringing continued. It was the phone. She switched on the bedside light and checked her watch; it was four a.m. She pulled back the duvet, her heart beating rapidly against the wall of her chest. It could only be bad news. She felt quite dizzy. Charlotte, their eighteen-year-old daughter, was backpacking in Malaya. One of the headlines on the nine o'clock news that evening had been the 'killer smog' in Kuala Lumpur. She tore across the room and snatched up the receiver.

'Hello,' she said breathlessly.

'Kitty – it's me.' It was her husband Richard. He was in Hong Kong on business.

'Richard! Oh my God! What's wrong – are you ill?'

'No, no, I'm fine. Sorry to ring at this ungodly hour, but I've just remembered something terribly important.'

Relief flooded through her system as she lowered her tiny frame onto a chair. At forty-five Kitty was still a beautiful woman with jet black short cropped hair and vivid violet eyes.

'Darling, you know those guns and that gaudy little pistol

we've got stored in the box at the bank?'

Kitty shook her head in disbelief. 'Richard, I cannot believe you're ringing me at four o'clock in the morning to discuss *guns!*'

'No, now *listen* to me. They've got to be handed in to the police. I should have done it before I left.'

'Alright, if I get time I'll try and do it tomorrow.'

'You must *make* the time otherwise they won't pay the compensation. The gun amnesty ends at midnight tomorrow. Everything you need is in the box...'

The door to the bedroom opened and Giles lumbered, bleary-eyed, into the room. He stood staring at his mother questioningly. She in turn looked back at her son with despair; his girth seemed to be increasing daily; no wonder he was nicknamed 'Porky'. He had been a gorgeous roly-poly baby, a squidgy toddler, a plump boy but now, at thirteen, there was no denying it – he was 'fat'. She would enforce that diet tomorrow.

She cupped the receiver with her hand. 'It's Dad,' she mouthed. 'Everything's fine, go back to bed.'

Giles yawned, nodded and obediently left the room.

'Kit – have you been listening to a *word* I've said?' Richard sounded indignant.

'Sorry, Darling. Do go on,' Kitty said guiltily.

'So, if you don't hand them over we could be fined five thousand pounds or worse still thrown into jail!'

Kitty reassured her husband. 'Don't worry Richard, I'll do it first thing tomorrow.'

The following day, after collecting the guns from the security box in the bank, Kitty stood in line at Earlsfield Police Station in Garratt Lane. A more respectable queue of people you could not find, each clutching their individual weapons disguised in various bags. Richard's guns were in a freezer bag. The pistol was separate wrapped in tissue at the bottom of her handbag. She felt reluctant to hand it over.

It had once belonged to Ruby, her Irish grandmother who, as a girl, emigrated to the USA and became a nightclub singer in Chicago. A red-haired, green-eyed beauty, she was known as 'Ruby from the Emerald Isle' and carried the four-inch Smith and Wesson pistol concealed inside her stocking garter. It was a gift from an admirer and was decorated with a cluster of minute rubies and emeralds. Kitty had always meant to have it valued.

An hour later Kitty sat in a tiny room while the Firearms Officer, a gaunt looking man with a walrus moustache and bushy eyebrows silently inspected Richard's ice-cold guns: there were five in all. He squinted down each of the barrels before noting the details meticulously in a register.

'You are compensating, aren't you?' Kitty said, breaking the silence.

He looked across at her and nodded.

'They're worth quite a lot,' Kitty ventured.

He nodded again while placing the guns into two transparent evidence bags. When he'd finished he folded his hands and looked straight at her. 'Can I see your licence, please?'

Kitty looked at him blankly. 'Licence? But they're antique – you don't need a licence for antique guns.'

'You do if the guns are capable of firing. Do you have a licence, Madam?'

'No – but this is ridiculous! My husband's had the guns for years – he keeps them in the bank for God's sake.'

'I'm sorry, Madam but without a licence there is no compensation.'

Kitty pleaded, argued and finally burst into tears. 'But that's not fair – you can't just take them and give us nothing in return.'

'Madam,' he said decisively, 'I don't make the rules, I'm here to carry them out. I should also point out that you have been holding these guns *illegally*,' he brought the tips of his fingers together importantly, 'and could be prosecuted – no licence.'

Kitty stood up. 'I never thought I would come into a *British* Police station and be robbed,' she said, exaggerating her New York accent. 'I better go now before I say something I regret.' Head held high she walked to the door and opened it; then she remembered Ruby's pistol still lying at the bottom of her bag. She hesitated and turned.

'Is there something else Madam?'

Kitty blanched. 'Er... no... nothing else.'

Kitty could not wait to get home, her head was pounding. Not only had she been robbed but she felt like a criminal as well. What was she going do with Ruby's pistol? She phoned the art gallery she managed in Wimbledon to say she would not be coming in and then she set about finding a suitable hiding place. Under the mattress, inside a hat, beneath her sweaters, amongst her lingerie, but nowhere was right. She began to panic as she paced around the bedroom thinking hard.

The loft – of course- why didn't I think of that before? She darted out onto the landing and manoeuvred the ladder down. Clasping the pistol she started to climb up towards the gaping hole. And then she heard it – a crash. Kitty froze on the ladder. The noise had come from downstairs. It was only two o'clock, two hours before Giles was due home. Kitty descended the ladder and crept warily down the stairs where she stood listening in the hall; from the kitchen she could definitely hear someone moving around. The crash she heard would have been them breaking in. Should she bolt out of the front door and call for help? Just then a low grinding noise started up, the sound of a drill. There was a small wall-safe in the breakfast room where she kept her jewellery. Fury suddenly coursed through Kitty's veins; one daylight robbery was enough! She looked at Ruby's pistol still in her hand and felt a surge of power. Holding it out in front of her she approached the kitchen door and in one decisive movement leant forward, grabbed it open and stepped in.

'Whatever you're doing – freeze!' she shouted.

There was a yell followed by a clang. Kitty stood staring at her son. On the table in front of him an upturned, still revolving electric egg whisk growled relentlessly against the side of a bowl filled with trembling, stiffened egg whites. Large dollops of the mixture spewed upwards landing unceremoniously on Giles' already ashen face.

'What the hell do you think you're doing – I thought you were a burglar?' Kitty angrily surveyed the table littered with eggshells, melted chocolate in a bowl, a broken glass dish lying shattered on the tiled floor and a Delia Smith cookery book standing up on end.

'Co-Cooking – Mum!' His eyes were wide with fear.

'You're supposed to be at school!' shouted Kitty, quivering with rage.

'Mum!' Giles repeated, his voice an octave higher as he pointed at her hand. She looked and saw with horror that she was aiming the pistol at him with her finger on the trigger. She gasped and threw it sideways on to the floor. Mother and son looked guiltily at each other.

That evening, relaxing in the sitting room after supper, there was an uncomfortable truce between them. The pistol, which she'd locked up in the safe, had acquired an ominous presence in the house. Giles was strangely silent. She'd tried to justify to him why she had kept the pistol recounting her experience with the arms officer earlier that day. He'd listened, scowling deeply, his chin resting in his pudgy hands and then he'd said, 'Would you have shot me if I'd been a burglar, Mum?'

'Of course not, don't be silly. It was just a threat.' Kitty wished she'd been as certain as she'd sounded.

'Does it work?'

'I shouldn't think so for a minute – it's antique.'

'Did it work – once?' Giles had persisted.

'Ye-es – I suppose so.'

'So *why* wouldn't it work now?'

'I don't know – but I'm sure it doesn't.' The questions rattled Kitty. 'I don't want to discuss it any more, Giles, but what I do want to discuss is why *you* weren't at school today?'

He'd shrugged, informing her that it was only games he had missed. The new sports teacher made him run which caused much jocularity from the other boys.

'So,' Kitty said, not too unkindly, 'you decided to come home instead and fill your face with chocolate mousse?'

'I did not – I came home to cook, it's the only thing I'm good at. I hate games, they're a waste of time.' Giles' burning ambition was to become a chef. Unlike other boys his age his bedroom was stacked high with cookery books and posters of the Two Fat Ladies adorned his walls.

'Games are good for you, they make you into a more rounded person,' Kitty said reasonably.

'According to you, Mum, I'm rounded enough already!'

'You know I'm going to have to tell your Father about this,

don't you?'

Giles nodded. 'And I'm going to have to tell him about you too Mum.'

Kitty uncrossed her legs and looked at him.

'You're putting us all in danger with that horrid gun.' He stood up. 'Now, I'd better finish that chocolate mousse.' His expression was both sly and challenging.

At ten o'clock that night Kitty came to a decision.

Half an hour later she and Giles walked into Earlsfield Police station and were shown into the little room. It was the same Firearms Officer who looked wearily up at her.

'Yes, Madam, did you forget something?'

'Actually, ye-es.' Kitty fumbled in her bag and withdrew Ruby's pistol. She handed it across to him. She could feel herself blushing as she prattled on nonsensically about finding it in the loft. Giles shifted from foot to foot with embarrassment and the Officer looked bored.

He studied the pistol carefully; he then looked up and held it out to Kitty. 'It's a replica Madam, incapable of firing, you can have it back.' He didn't even smile but added, coldly looking at his watch, 'You have an hour left to remember any *other* items that just may have slipped your memory; after that you will be charged with an offence.'

They giggled helplessly on the journey back and when they got home Kitty went into the sitting room and poured herself a double brandy.

Giles disappeared into the kitchen returning a minute later with two large servings of chocolate mousse. He handed one to Kitty who was about to protest when he stopped her.

'We've got to eat it Mum because tomorrow I start my diet.

No more mousse till - till next time!' He grinned cheekily but she knew he meant it.

Next day Kitty returned Ruby's pistol to the box in the bank. She was about to close the lid when she noticed an envelope lying at the bottom. She took it out; there was writing on the front in Richard's hand. She read, *Current Gun Licence - 1997.* Kitty dropped it back inside and slowly closed the lid. Tomorrow Richard was returning home, she would face the music then.

FOL-DE-ROL

The horse gazed unflinchingly at Felix from the chair where it was sitting in the centre of the room, its motionless head lit by the early morning light seeping through the attic window above. The object of its gaze turned over in the rickety double bed, raised himself up on one elbow and peered back across the dimly lit room.

'I don't suppose you slept a wink, frolicked your way through the night as usual, always were perverse, arse about face. Well you can't stop in bed today my love, today we've got things to do.' Felix eased himself up, folded the bedclothes neatly back, then slowly swivelled on his bottom till his short, stubby legs were dangling over the edge of the bed, his toes contemplating the cold brown lino beneath him. He raised one buttock, gently breaking wind and glanced guiltily over at the horse.

'Don't look so superior, it's better out than in, that's what I say, and we aren't all blessed with your self-control.'

His feet searched out his well-worn slippers before he slowly straightened up massaging his back with little 'oohs!' and 'aahs!' He turned to face the bed and started burrowing beneath the bedding, withdrew a perished pink hot-water bottle and placed on the bedside table. Then, with one well-practised movement, he pulled all the bedclothes back again, smoothing out the creases with his pudgy fingers and with a final flourish plumped up the pillows.

'There! That's done! Not to your high standards I will admit,' he addressed the horse while reaching for his dressing gown which was hanging from the bed-post, 'but good enough for me. I'm not as fussy as you, can't see the point of making it all neat and tidy only to mess it all up again.' Felix hugged himself. 'Brrrr! More like January than November.'

He shuffled over to the window, drew the curtains back and let the grey day in. He then proceeded to the fireplace, stroking the head of the horse affectionately on the way, retrieved some matches from the mantelpiece and lit the small gas fire. He stood quite still for several moments warming his backside against the heat staring sadly at the familiar back, its ears alert and projecting above the seat. Finally, Felix cleared his throat.

'There's something I've got to tell you, can't keep it to myself no more.' He took a deep breath before continuing. 'They're throwing me out, see, say I can't look after myself, there've been complaints – other people in the house – they say I keep them awake at night talking to myself. I explained to them that I wasn't talking to myself, that I was talking to you.' Felix chuckled shaking his head from side to side. 'You should see their faces when I mention you; they look at me like I'm dulally!'

He sat down in the shabby armchair next to the fire. 'Sheltered housing, that's what they call it – that's where they're sending me though I'm not sure what I'm being sheltered from.'

Felix looked over towards the horse then dropped his head and stared sadly at the floor. He spoke very quietly

'No love, I can't take you, "no domestics", they said. I pleaded with Mrs. Botting. She's my social worker, says I can call her Beatrix but I won't. I call her Mrs. Botting, she calls you *Horsey*! "You can't possibly take Horsey, Felix, he's far too big and cumbersome." That's how she talks,' said Felix, imitating a woman's rather well-educated tones, his own distinct, rural sounds momentarily forgotten.

'I know you'd have told her where to get off, but I'm not like you Rolly – you never gave a tinker's cuss what people thought – I longed to be like you.'

Felix stared into the fire remembering fondly the day Rolly, Roland Gilbert, the 'G' pronounced softly, exploded into his life.

They were manacled together with handcuffs on a disused, wind-swept railway station platform in Suffolk, wearing pinstriped suits and bowler hats. It was a commercial for some new-fangled car and they were extras or 'Background Artistes', as Felix preferred to be called, depicting the horrors of the commuting businessman. There were twenty-five of them that day, all chained together.

Felix had first noticed Roland on their arrival early in the morning; a coach had brought them down from London. They were in a large tent erected in a field. Roland was standing aloof from Felix and the other extras who were tucking into the free breakfast provided, their plates piled high, not an inch of space wasted. He was eating an apple, wearing a Russian-style fur coat and hat accentuating his Slavic cheekbones and aristocratic features; everything about him was statuesque except his height; he was tiny, cleverly concealed by high platform shoes.

Felix decided he must be an actor. They rarely acknowledged the extras, let alone spoke to them.

No one was more surprised than Felix to find out later that he was, in fact, just one of them.

It had been a gruelling morning, the light had been playing up, one of the cameras had broken down and tempers had generally been frayed. They had been standing, chained, for close on three hours without a break, their hands blue with cold, their wrists sore and their feet numb.

They were being filmed from the opposite platform.

The first assistant, a short, mean looking man with a pockmarked face and a renowned bad temper, shouted 'Cut!' He then turned his back on the line of extras and addressed the crew. 'Take a break now, fellers. I should get in there first before we let this lot loose.' He indicated the extras with a derogatory nod of his head and snorted. 'At least we've got them tethered! That must be a first!' He turned to face the line of fettered men, some of whom had heard his comments and yelled in bored tones across the line: 'Gentlemen, if we could ask you to be patient, I'm letting the crew go first for lunch. They've got to be back before your good selves to set up for this afternoon. Thank you.'

Roland turned and looked at Felix, his muscles had gone taut and his face was twitching with rage. 'You're not going to let him get away with that, are you? It's outrageous!'

That was the first thing Felix heard him say. His voice was rich and classless. Felix, not quite sure how to respond to this, shrugged in a helpless manner.

'Well I'm certainly not!' Roland then stepped forward as far as the fetters would allow him. 'Excuse me,' his voice boomed out and reverberated around the station.

The first assistant stopped in his tracks and turned to see from where the voice had come, his look indicating the displeasure he felt at being disturbed. 'Yes? What is it?'

Roland spoke clearly and with a quiet authority. 'You're not seriously going to leave us here while you go off to lunch?'

You could have heard a pin drop in that station. The crew stepped back to see what was gong on, all the other extras watched this new man in their midst with growing admiration.

'You obviously weren't listening. I'm letting the crew go first so...'

'We all heard you loud and clear,' said Roland, cutting in. 'And I'm demanding that you undo these chains immediately, otherwise I, for one, will not return this afternoon.'

There was a general murmur of approval from the men standing in the line. The first assistant stepped to the edge of the platform, both hands on his hips, his face white with rage. 'Who are you?' he hissed menacingly.

'Roland Gilbert,' replied Roland, pronouncing the 'Gilbert' in the French way. 'And who are you?'

Felix's stomach lurched at the daring of this man.

'Mike Dakin, and I am the first assistant. You, obviously, are new and haven't yet learnt that what I say goes around here and you'll do what I bloody well say! Comprenez, Monsieur *Gilbert*?'

'And you, Mister Dakin, have usurped your authority by keeping us tied up here. We are cold, uncomfortable and our bladders are full. I suggest most strongly that you release us now if you want any of us to return this afternoon.'

There was a chorus of 'hear hears' from the other extras, at first starting quietly, but gathering momentum as their courage grew. Even Felix, normally so timid, decided to join in.

The two men stood glaring at each other across the track, inextricably divided. By this time a large crowd had gathered on the platform, including the director and some worried-looking men from the advertising agency. Somebody called Mike's name sharply. He walked back and was immediately immersed in a huddle of muted mutterings, resulting in the third assistant being dispatched post-haste to undo the tethered men. A general cheer went up and Roland became the hero of the day. Mike Dakin was defeated.

'So?' said Felix, thrilled to be sitting next to Roland on the long coach journey home that night. 'Why haven't we seen you round before?'

'Because this was my first day as an extra,' Roland paused, 'and definitely my last, I'd rather clean toilets!'

Felix laughed. 'Oh, they're not all like that. We usually have a good laugh, days like today you just have to switch off, think of the money and enjoy the food!' He patted his bulging belly. 'Trouble is I enjoy mine too much!'

Roland glanced down at Felix's stomach disapprovingly. 'I'm very careful what I eat but then in my job you have to be.'

'Oh, what's that?' said Felix, trying desperately to draw his stomach in.

'I'm a circus acrobat – on a horse.'

Felix's eyes grew large. 'Ooh, how exciting, I love the circus. Are you between jobs then?'

Roland stared straight ahead. 'No, the circus I was with went into liquidation.

'But can't you join another circus?'

Roland laughed bitterly. 'At my age? We live in a youth-fixated society, though I can outride any one of them!'

Felix was fascinated by Roland's nose; his flared nostrils appeared to palpitate when he was angry.

'Besides, the receivers took my horses. I couldn't afford to buy them back…' His voice trailed off and he looked studiously out of the window into the blackness of the night.

During the course of the journey Felix discovered that Roland was not only horseless, but homeless too. He was staying with Rita Star in her pokey basement flat behind Olympia, sleeping on a camp bed in a room shared by Rita, her Pekinese, two Persian cats and a very noisy parrot. Felix knew Rita well. She had been one of the Seven Shooting Stars, an acrobatic act, but was now retired and earned her living as an extra and part-time gardener.

As they talked Felix felt a strange sense of destiny with this proud but helpless man and heard himself saying, 'You can come and stay with me till you get sorted out, it's nothing grand, but it's light and airy.'

Roland turned to look at Felix, searching his face for any trace of insincerity. He suddenly smiled and Felix's heart stood still.

Roland moved in the next day, his face lighting up as he entered the large attic room. He paced around it like a matador in the ring. 'But this is wonderful, Felix, you can do so much with it!'

Felix, who'd been living there ten years, smiled. He wasn't hurt, he knew his life had just begun.

Felix pulled his gaze away from the fire, stood up, went over to the horse and boxed it playfully on the ear. 'And you never went away, did you?' He walked over to a large mahogany wardrobe, removed a navy suit and various accessories which he then laid neatly on the bed, before collecting a sponge-bag and towel from a marble washstand in the corner of the room. 'Well I'm off to have a scrub a-dub-dub, shan't be long.'

Felix left the room, returning twenty minutes later pink and gleaming. He stood in the doorway; a wave of emotion sweeping over him as he gazed at the horse in the full morning light for the last time. He shut the door leaning up against it and remembered the first time.

He and Roland had been living harmoniously together for six months. Roland was working at the Queen's Theatre in the box office. 'Only temporarily,' he told Felix, a mysterious grin on his face. 'I have a plan.'

Felix returned home one day feeling queasy after ten long hours of chewing chicken nuggets for a commercial; they had chewed in time to music and his jaw was aching. He had opened the door. The room was dark. He had switched on the light and nearly jumped out of his skin to see a horse sitting there with its legs provocatively crossed and, when it opened its mouth, it spoke with a southern belle drawl.

'Well, hello there, you must be the feline Felix all the gals have been telling me about!'

'Rolly?' Felix gaped at the horse. 'Is that you?'

The horse shook its head and sighed. 'My name is Fol-de-Rol, I'm not a feller, I'm a filly!' It batted its eyelids coyly, fluttering its long lashes.

Felix giggled foolishly.

Suddenly Roland's head emerged as he removed the horse's head and held it out gleefully to Felix like an excited child.

He then scrambled out of the equine legs and announced, 'You and I, Felix, are going to be the most famous, the funniest and the most fantastical filly in the business!'

Felix's early reservations about becoming the back end of a horse were soon overcome, and for four months they pounded and paced around the attic room rehearsing the act.

Sometimes they were overseen by Rita Star and Petal, her Pekinese, who went into a sexual frenzy whenever Fol-de-Rol appeared and had to be tied up to the bedpost. Roland was a tireless teacher; perfection was his aim and thus *Fol-de-Rol the Flirtatious Filly* was launched.

They made their debut at Hampstead Fair, drawing a large and delighted crowd around them. Rita, wearing a top hat and traditional ringmaster's gear, the scarlet jacket clashing violently with her bright red wig, worked the music. When the act was over she strode around flourishing her whip and collecting money in her hat. Each weekend that summer they found a different fair or fete and, on the weekdays in between, they honed and polished up the act. That autumn they were booked for *Babes in the Woods* at the Hippodrome, Eastbourne, and within a short space of time they were constantly in demand.

Felix let out a contented sigh; those were the happiest seven years of his life. In his youth he had failed miserably as an actor, stage fright being the cause, but Fol-de-Rol had given him approval and applause yet in the comfort of anonymity.

It all came to an abrupt end one day in June. They had been at Spotlight signing their biggest contract to date: a Christmas Special at the Pavilion Theatre, Bournemouth. Roland had been strangely quiet and suggested calling a taxi to take them home; once inside the cab he started twisting and turning, tearing frantically at his clothes, his face puce, he couldn't breathe. The taxi driver turned, took one look at him, put his foot down on the accelerator and drove at full speed to the nearby Middlesex Hospital. On their arrival Roland's heart had stopped beating and the medics worked at resuscitating him unceremoniously in the hospital corridor. For three days Roland's life hung in the balance and the faithful Felix barely left his side. 'Malignant Hypertension' they called it: extreme high blood pressure with heart and kidney complications. When finally he did pull through a quiet and stress-free life was prescribed, along with vital life saving drugs to be taken daily without fail. Fol-de-Rol was banished to a box on top of the wardrobe and Felix took up extra work again.

The euphoria of being alive soon wore off; Roland had a low boredom threshold; the attic was strewn with half-started paintings, unfinished poems, books on philosophy and the meaning of life dipped into but little understood. Roland's education had been scant. He became morose and self-absorbed and talked of going to New Zealand to join his brother who had a small stud farm just outside Wellington. Inwardly Felix wept but he started a 'Wellington fund' collecting coins in an old gumboot he kept standing in the hearth.

As Roland grew stronger so his depression deepened, the lines in his handsome face were etched in sadness; like a proud stallion whose spirit had finally been broken, Felix had inwardly reflected. He took to going out alone at night returning in the early hours of the morning to sleep the day away. Felix never asked him where he went and Roland never told him.

'I never slept when you went out,' said Felix, crossing the room and starting to dress himself, taking meticulous care. 'I suppose I was scared that one day you'd just walk out into the night and disappear and I'd never see you again.'

He sat down on the bed and polished his shoes before putting them on. Then he slid open the bedside drawer and took out a shallow rectangular box and removed the lid. Lying inside on white tissue were two identical silk ties, one in red, the other in blue, with all the letters of Fol-de-Rol jumbled up in the opposing colour. Felix selected the blue one with red letters; leaving the box on the bed he walked over to the long mirror on the wall and carefully knotted the tie. Roland, who was extravagant with money, had them designed to celebrate the fifth anniversary of

Fol-de-Rol's conception. That had been a good year, money in the bank and their first holiday abroad together. Felix stepped back and surveyed himself critically. He wet his fingers with his tongue and smoothed the white hair down surrounding the shiny, pink dome of his head. He turned to face Fol-de-Rol and let out a long, deep, shuddering sigh.

'That's it, my love, can't put if off no longer.'

He walked quickly away from the horse, climbed on the bed and reached up for a large oblong box resting on top of the wardrobe. He swayed unsteadily on the spongy mattress before lowering himself and the box to the ground. He carried it over to Fol-de-Rol and placed it on the floor, took off the lid; the lower half of the horse lay inertly inside. Felix gently lifted Fol-de-Rol by the neck; the front legs dangled pathetically in front as he reverently and lovingly laid her in the box. The eyes of the filly rolled back and stared vacantly up at the ceiling. Felix fetched the red tie and kneeling on the floor he draped it round the neck.

'There, there,' he said, stroking the head soothingly. 'There, there, my love. You go to sleep now.'

He leant forward and kissed her on the forelock before he tenderly pulled each eye firmly closed. He stood up, his body shaking with emotion as he put the lid hastily back on the box. He walked over to the window and stood waiting and watching, remembering that fateful Sunday afternoon in November two years before.

He had been to the launderette and was expecting to find Roland still asleep, but as he'd opened the front door of the house he heard his voice calling down excitedly. 'Where're you been, for God's sake?'

'Where do you think I've been?' said Felix proffering the

laundry bags and plodding up the stairs. 'Dancing?'

'How can any one take so long coming up the stairs!?' Roland said impatiently before pushing Felix into the attic and springing out in front of him, grinning from ear to ear.

'What's got into you?' said Felix. 'You look like a cat who's licked the cream!'

'Not the cream,' Roland replied and leapt on to the arm of the armchair, 'but the crème de la crème!' With that he leapt through the air, landing on the arm of the second chair. Felix watched in amazement. Roland's face was sizzling with energy, the years had dropped away.

'Guess what!'

'What? We've won the pools?' Felix guessed.

'Don't be such a philistine, Felix! How do you fancy appearing before Her Majesty the Queen tonight at The Royal Variety Show?'

'Don't be daft!' said Felix, sinking on the bed with the laundry.

'It's true. Sam Small needs a horse, we've been asked to step in at the last minute.'

'Sam Small! He's that vulgar, fat comic!'

'Yes him,' replied Roland.

'He's singing a song dressed up as the fastest and fattest cowboy in the West, but every time he mounts his faithful horse he flattens it!'

'I'm not surprised!' said Felix wryly. 'He must weigh twenty stone. He probably killed his other horse! Anyway the answer's no!'

Roland's face crumpled as he jumped down and came over to Felix pleadingly. 'Oh please, Felix, just this once?'

'No, Rolly. You know what the doctors said - if you want to

live then...'

Roland stopped him. 'Wrong Felix, I shall die if you won't let me do it. Shirley Bassey's topping the bill and we'll be on stage with her at the finale! Just imagine!'

Felix felt himself weakening. Shirley Bassey was their idol; against his better judgement he reluctantly agreed.

Forty minutes later a black limousine collected them and, together with Fol-de-Rol, they were transported to the Palladium. Sam Small greeted them eagerly. Not a moment to lose he whisked them off to the circle bar, his three chins wobbling as they went, to run through the routine. They had missed the dress rehearsal but were allowed ten minutes up on stage rehearsing with the orchestra and being given their positions for the grand finale. There was half an hour till curtain up.

The air was charged with chaos and excitement. Famous faces flitted past them as they were being shown to the tiny dressing room they were to share with a magician from Hungary who suffered from B.O. and smoked incessantly, his giggling twin assistants and a flock of white doves.

'All we need now is Rita's parrot!' Roland observed.

The routine had gone well. Felix wasn't crushed to death as he had feared and Fol-de-Rol got bigger laughs than Sam Small and a huge round of applause as she trotted off the stage. Sam had hugged them both and called them 'true professionals'.

Afterwards they sat quietly in the dressing room, listening to the other acts over the Tannoy system and waiting to be called for the finale line-up. They had all been given positions on the stairs where they were to wait; strict precision was necessary to avoid a stampede. Shirley Bassey began to sing 'My Way' when the call came.

Felix and Roland looked at each other rapturously as they left the dressing-room and took up their places on the steps; Sam Small came out and stood between them, the Croatian Boy's Choir was lined up behind, the Magician and his girls were just ahead. Felix, who was in front, peeped around Sam's bulky body at Roland, who was standing clasping Fol-de-Rol's head, his face flushed with excitement. A young man rushed into view with his arm held high in the air; he lowered it dramatically and they started to move down the stairs towards the stage.

They were in the second row, Felix was right behind Shirley Bassey, her gown was a shimmering sheath of gold. He was dazzled. The curtain rose and fell to tumultuous applause and then the orchestra struck up, the audience all stood, and the entire cast turned to face the Royal Box and sang 'God Save the Queen'. Felix's spine tingled, he turned towards Roland – he wasn't there. Felix looked frantically further down the line; the juices of his mouth ran dry and his heart beat wildly – Roland wasn't there. Before the anthem finished he ran down the row of startled artists into the wings, then up the three flights of stairs towards the dressing room.

Roland was sitting on the top step his head slumped forward with Fol-de-Rol at his feet.

That was the last time Felix saw Roland.

'No fuss, no funerals for me,' he had announced when he was ill. 'I'm bequeathing my body to medical science.'

Alone in the room later that night Felix could not face the unmade bed; the scent of Roland still fresh upon the pillow. Instead he sat huddled by the hearth in the forlorn hope of hearing Rolly's footsteps creeping up the stairs. When they didn't come agony turned to guilt and anger at himself for allowing Fol-de-Rol to perform. He suddenly grabbed the Wellington boot and hurled it violently across the room, the coins cascaded out along with myriads of tiny white pills – Roland's life-saving pills which spun and spiralled their way around the floor. When the last one subsided Felix sat down again and sobbed, his heart broken by the depth of his friend's despair.

Two loud honks made Felix look out of the window where Rita was emerging from her lime green mini-van with its moss-encrusted windows. She waved up to him and he noted with approval that she was wearing her black Cleopatra wig. Rolly used to joke that Rita's hair was worn away by all those feet once climbing up upon her head.

They slid Fol-de-Rol's box into the back of the van and then they drove the long journey in silence only interrupted by Petal who whined and scrabbled frantically at the box. Rita drove with both hands gripping the wheel, knuckles white, a cigarette clamped sideways in her mouth, the spiral of smoke causing her one eye to permanently water.

When they reached the New Forest Felix gave directions to a spot that he had known as a child. There they parked the car. Felix removed the box and Rita took out a large, man-sized spade and a rucksack. Petal bounded in front of them as they walked deep into the forest their footsteps crunching the autumn leaves.

Under a tree, where the earth was soft, Rita began to dig, her wig shifting violently with each mighty thrust of the spade, refusing all offers of help from Felix. 'This is my job,' she told him gruffly.

Petal held up the procedure by leaping into the hole then

leaping out again, shaking and showering them with earth; eventually they tied her to a tree. Halfway through the digging Rita produced some sandwiches which they silently munched, sharing a bottle of Guinness to wash them down. She resumed her work with the same relentless yet joyless fervour. When she'd finished she nodded grimly at Felix. She rested her spade against a tree and together, they lifted Fol-de-Rol's box and lowered it carefully into the newly dug grave. Rita walked back, collected the spade and handed it solemnly to Felix, who stood staring down at the box, a look of yearning on his face, before he bravely scooped up some earth and sprinkled it on top. Rita took over, filling the grave quickly and efficiently and finally flattening the earth with the back of her spade. That done she fetched a small tape player from her rucksack, placed it on the ground and switched it on. She walked back to Felix and took his arm. Shirley Bassey's voice boomed out 'My Way', accompanied by Petal, who began to howl mournfully. And when, in the song, it came to '*Is this the final curtain*?' Rita's stoic self-control gave way and she too began to howl, comforted by Felix who was relieved to share his grief though his own tears were still locked away inside him. After the song had ended and the shattered peace of the forest was restored, Felix knelt down, and with his finger, pierced holes in the shape of a horseshoe on top of the grave. Rita stepped forward and handed him some tiny bulbs which he then delicately planted.

The ceremony over, the mourners returned to the mini-van led by Petal, who callously scampered in front of them. They drove out of the forest into the lightness of open, undulating moorland with its fierce, stubby looking gorse bushes.

Felix suddenly pulled urgently at Rita's sleeve. 'Rita, Rita, please stop!'

She pulled up on the verge and Felix scrambled out of the van and ran diagonally back across the road to where a small black horse was standing, its head held high. Felix stared into the deep, brown, liquid eyes.

'Thank you, Rolly. I needed to see you just one more time. I'm letting you go, see, you don't have to worry about me no more, you're a free spirit now.'

The horse stepped nearer. Felix felt his eyes begin to blur, hot coals burned in his throat. 'Go on now, love. I'm setting you free!'

When the horse didn't move he put both hands out and shoved it away roughly.

'Go on now – bugger off!'

Startled, the horse trotted back a short distance, stopped, looked at Felix and then galloped off across the moorland.

Felix, his tears flowing freely now, watched until it became but a speck of dust on the horizon. He raised his hand in a final farewell.

REFLECTED
GLORY

I was, please note the past tense, a thing of exquisite beauty. I arrived in a swathe of tissue paper incarcerated in a box and was presented to my mistress on her betrothal. Please don't ask me what that is, but the words *To Daisy May on the occasion of her betrothal to Sir Randolph Parker, April 1911* are indelibly inscribed on my back. It was love at first sight. She picked me up and gazed at me so tenderly and with such infinite pleasure, that I could feel myself steaming up and the vision of her delicate face faded in to a hazy blur until, softly and gently, she wiped me down with a small white square of material impregnated with her fragrance. We spent many hours together and, without appearing to sound conceited or narcissistic, she worshiped me. I suppose I should mention here the imposter who accompanied me in the box on that memorable day; the markings on his back were, I reluctantly admit, impressive and more intricate than mine but there all comparisons must end. He was unspeakably coarse and hairy and probably from a bazaar in Bombay. I tried my utmost to have as little to do with him as possible.

Those early times were the happy times, the times when she reached out to me for my approval, holding me in the air while she dragged the imposter through the thick mane of burnished brown hair that framed her perfect oval face. This ritual completed, she would smile bewitchingly at me, her lips quivering in anticipation as she gently teased them with tapered fingers before placing me aside. Brightness turned to darkness and then the sighs, the moans, the joyous rhythmic cries, the words *Randolph oh Randolph*, the terrible grunts and groans before silence restored the harmony of the room.

I did not care for the master and he had little time for me; occasionally we would come face to face when he would stare at me long and hard, then sneer, he didn't smile. He had the strange habit of stroking his black moustache, tweaking it upwards and flaring his nostrils disdainfully as though I smelt, but I returned his gaze with equal candour. I have a talent for mimicry, you see, and there's no one I cannot imitate, however mighty, except when darkness falls and my gift no longer works. I suffer from night-blindness, a weakness I rarely talk about.

Little did I know in those early days how dramatically my status was going to change. It seemed to coincide with the long absence of the master. My last glimpse of him, he was wearing on his head an extraordinary black pointed cap with golden metal on the front and a red box on top from which protruded a massive black plume. His chest was clad in a bright crimson jacket with bold brass buttons running up on either side. Even I will admit that he looked very dashing, though his appearance caused my mistress to weep and, in between tears, to say *Oh Randolph, please, please don't go!*

During this period my mistress spent less time with me, the gleam had gone from her eyes; she would look soulfully through me rather than at me and, instead of smiling, she'd sigh and push me away face downwards. I cannot function on my face. I feel helpless, the purpose of my being is extinguished, to live without a purpose is nothing short of purgatory.

Events went from bad to worse and began with a wail of lament from my mistress of such intensity and despair that all of us in the room shook in unison. She did not communicate with me for days on end and when she did she shocked me to the core: the once lustrous hair hung limply down, her face had become gaunt and pale, deep blue valleys ran beneath her bloodshot eyes. She looked at me with utter loathing. Why did she no longer need me? What heinous deed had I committed to cause my fall from grace?

My only comfort came from an ugly creature whose head was covered in a frilly white cloth cap. She had eyes that met in the middle which I found quite disconcerting and a large nose which she insisted on showing to me. It was covered in tiny black dots which she tried, unsuccessfully, to extract but which left her nose blotchy and red. However, she showed me real affection and would cover me in a delicious cool cream which she would sensuously stroke into me; no place was left untouched and then the rubbing would begin which both hurt and pleasured me until I shone, my original beauty restored. She never bothered with the imposter, who was showing his real colour and turning black. Sadly I spent much of this time bundled in a drawer with barely enough light for reflection. It was a ghastly period.

Just when I had given up all hope of ever seeing the light again, my mistress decided to bestow her favours on me once more, indeed the fickle lady began to flirt with me and I could not resist. The bloom was fully restored to her cheeks, the hair was short and wavy now clamped closely to her head and the look in her eyes was, how can I describe it? Knowing? She would arch an eyebrow at me, half smile, willing me to do the same. I had no choice but to reciprocate so great was my fear of banishment. The nocturnal noises returned to the room again but were somehow less restrained. *Edward, Edward!* my mistress would shriek.

And then, on that fateful morning, when the light had slipped into the room and I was waiting to greet my mistress, I felt an unfamiliar grasp as I whirled through the air and was placed into the hand of my mistress. She smiled sleepily up at me, her head resting on a lacy white pillow.

'By Gad, you're beautiful, look at yourself,' a deep voice said. 'Watch me while I worship you.'

I moved down her unclad body viewing sights I'd never seen before, and was surprised to see nestling between her milky white thighs a head with flaxen hair. My position was untenable. The head lifted up and I was confronted with a pair of ice blue eyes and bloated lips that leered.

But before I could compose myself there was the sound of a door bursting open and a human roar of rage.

My mistress stifled me flat against her beating breast crying out, 'Randolph! Oh Randolph, they told me you were dead.'

'You, Sir!' It was my master's voice. 'Stand up! Prepare to face your Maker like a man!'

The commotion grew louder. My mistress was screaming as I suddenly felt myself whisked upwards high into the air before plunging downwards on to my master's head over and over again, each crack louder than the one before. I could not stop myself, the sound of my master's final cry splintered my inner core. I was helpless, warm red liquid covered my face in shame. It was a shattering experience and one from which I will never recover.

'We must get rid of it.' Those were the last words I heard my mistress whisper.

Shortly after I entered a long dark tunnel where I failed to exist – or so I thought.

'Fuck me! Sharon look! Look what I dug up!'

I could barely make him out, so impaired was my vision, but he appeared to have a gold ring through his nose and another through his lip.

He seemed quite pleased to see me. 'Here Sharon, this might be worth a bob or two, looks like solid silver – it's dated and all. I'm goin' to fix it up.'

What happened to me next is too painful to recount, but suffice it to say I became a tawdry shadow of my former self, condemned to lie in a dusty window alongside vulgar jugs with faces, badly cut glass, deceased clocks, china cats, cracked plates and tarnished frames – even the imposter would have been an improvement on these inferior objects.

I who have always craved the light, found myself yearning for darkness and oblivion – and then I met my present master.

A bell tinkled and a few seconds later I was gently lifted up and found myself facing a white haired man with a pointed beard. He spent so long inspecting me through a magnifying glass that I became quite uncomfortable until I heard him say, 'Alec, look at this – it belonged to Lady Daisy May – I've just been reading up about her. She was condemned to death with her lover for murdering her husband.'

'Really darling,' a man's voice replied. 'How did they kill him?'

'Bludgeoned him to death, poor sod. They never found the instrument that did it.'

'Perhaps you're holding it in your hand – think of that!' The bearded man looked at me suspiciously – I had been found out.

'Don't be silly, dear heart, this wouldn't have the strength.'

I am now in a beautiful glass cabinet, looked after tenderly by Alec and Darling, the bearded man. Sometimes, when they have friends to dinner, they pass me round the table and talk endlessly about my mistress and her lover, speculating on how the dastardly deed was done, and I am quite content to remain silent and bask in their reflected glory.

The BEAUTIFUL COUPLE

Dennis snapped his book shut and slammed it down on the table. It wasn't till he'd reached the final paragraph that he realised he had read it once before and hadn't enjoyed it much then either. 'Life's too short to read the same book twice!' he said out loud, glancing across at Marjorie engrossed in the latest Rose Tremain novel.

'Nonsense, she said, barely looking up. 'I've read some of my favourite books dozens of times.'

'Not Dick Francis surely?' he said.

They were sitting high up on the terrace of the Hostailillo Hotel looking down on the idyllic pine clad cove of Tamariu on the Northern Costa Brava. The heat was intense and beads of perspiration had broken out beneath the strands of Dennis' thinning hair. He had refused to wear the hat Marjorie had waved at him after breakfast. It was forty years since they had last been here on their honeymoon but it could have been yesterday; nothing had changed except, Dennis looked mournfully across at his wife, themselves.

She was wearing a large straw hat, her prominent nose covered in a white paste like substance. She was nearly sixty-one; her tall shapely figure was swathed in an orange, silk sarong which showed off her still magnificent upright breasts. Marjorie's long bony fingers dangled possessively over the olive bowl. Periodically she would swipe one up and pop it into her mouth chewing and gnawing her way around the stone using her front teeth like a hamster. Dennis watched the olive routine with horrified fascination waiting for the moment she would spit the stone clear over the terrace wall. Another stone whizzed through the air.

'I wish you'd stop doing that with those stones – it's disgusting.'

'No one can see me,' she replied airily.

That was true. The terrace was now empty; the other guests must have moved to the pool or gone down to the beach.

He leaned back in his chair, stretched out his legs, blew out his cheeks and started to puff, the puffing turned into Prokofiev's *Dance of the Knights* - so confrontational. He could feel Marjorie's irritation. Good. He moved his sandaled feet up and down in time to the music until he caught sight of his new long shorts. He looked at them despairingly; he should never have let her talk him into buying them. Shorts should be short. These were longs, he looked like a boy scout. Why oh why had he agreed to come away with her? She hadn't taken her nose out of that book since they got here. This was his idea of hell. Too much time to sit and bloody think.

For the past ten years they had taken their holidays separately; Marjorie with the Ramblers Association and he with his golfing chums – an arrangement they had both been happy with, or so he had thought, until last March.

He had come down to breakfast surprised to find Marjorie in tears; these days she rarely showed emotion, that side of her closed down after their tragedy. *The Daily Telegraph* was spread out on the table, the obituary page lay open. She had pointed to the picture of a pleasant looking man by the name of

Robin Cairncross, a well-known ornithologist who, at the age of fifty-five, had died suddenly of a heart attack leaving behind a wife and two teenage children. Dennis had failed at first to see the significance of this event until Marjorie had pointed out that he was one of the 'ramblers'. He found himself wondering why she had never spoken of him before, but something told him to let the matter drop. A few days later she announced her rambling days were over, she was getting too old for all that sort of thing and why didn't they have a holiday together for a change? She seemed so enthusiastic almost begging him and he had foolishly agreed.

'Who knows,' she had said, 'maybe we can rekindle our relationship, or at least try.'

He doubted it; too much water under the bridge, too much hurt. He could never forget the way she had looked at him that night, eleven years ago, after they had heard the news. A look of undisguised hatred and recrimination on her face, and she was right. He too blamed himself. People deal with grief in different ways. He had not been much use to Marjorie; unable to comfort her, didn't understand why she had stayed with him. He hated himself too. Now they slept in separate rooms.

The heat was killing him. He took out his white handkerchief, knotted it into a square, placed it on top of his steaming head and returned to his thoughts. Things weren't that bad, they rarely argued, well, only about inconsequential matters, they often laughed at the same things and shared the same interests. He occasionally found solace with Connie, the kindly and comely widowed receptionist at his golf club. It was hardly a passionate relationship; Connie was undemanding and happy to comply on his terms. It suited them both. He didn't like deception but Marjorie would never know and probably wouldn't care if she did.

Marjorie looked up from her book and across at her fidgety husband aware that he was bored. The handkerchief on his head made him look like a day-tripper on Brighton Beach.

'Shall I get your hat?' she said brightly.

Dennis did not reply; he was distracted by the young couple walking down through the terraces hand in hand. They looked familiar. They were wearing shorts and T-shirts. The girl was no more than twenty, her blond streaked hair caught up in a ponytail, her face fresh and freckled. The man was older, Dennis guessed, could be 32. The familiar knot in his stomach tightened but he forced the thought away and watched the couple sit at the table directly in front of them on the lower terrace. He pointed them out to Marjorie. 'Look, it's that couple – they were on the table next to us last night at dinner. Ogled each other all through the meal – didn't even bother with dessert.'

Marjorie turned her gaze on them and nodded. 'Oh them.'

'They weren't at breakfast this morning either', he said knowingly, as he watched the young couple's hands joined together across the table, their fingers twining and intertwining, gaining in intensity.

'Who needs breakfast at their age?' Marjorie smiled, watching them.

'I always did,' Dennis replied.

'Not when we first came here – you weren't remotely interested in food.'

Dennis grunted. 'That was a long time ago.'

He had taken her virginity in this hotel and found that

Marjorie took to sex like a duck to water and was embarrassed by her own voracious appetite. They returned home pale but happy.

He remembered her as she was then, tall and self-effacing with a tremendous complex about her height. They had met at a regimental dance. He had spotted her sitting quietly on her own and plucked up courage, egged on by the other officers, to ask her for a dance. She declined sweetly complaining of a corn on her toe and then burst out laughing when he had said, 'Good – I can't dance anyway!' He had sat down beside her and they talked all evening. The attraction was instant and they made a date for his next term of leave.

She'd admitted later that she had declined to dance with him that night fearing her height might put him off.

'Titch,' he said suddenly, and chuckled

'What's that?' Marjorie looked at him.

'Titch – that's what I used to call you – I've just remembered.'

'Did you? Are you sure it wasn't "bitch"?' She smiled sardonically and pushed the olives in his direction. "Do have an olive, I'm sick of them." She returned to her book.

Dennis let his eyes wander back to the young couple. The girl was rubbing her calf against the man's leg and then delicately lifted her foot and with her bare toes teased her way along his thigh gently probing beneath his shorts.

'Good God!' Dennis exploded, 'Look what she's doing with her foot!'

'Dennis! Shush! They'll hear you.'

'No they won't. We're invisible to them.'

They sat in silence watching them. The couple removed their T-shirts. The girl stood up and handed the man a bottle of suntan cream.

'Look at her bikini,' Marjorie said. 'Polka dots – must be back in fashion.'

'Very brief,' Dennis said, feeling himself becoming aroused as he watched the young man massaging the cream into the girl's shapely bronzed back, his fingers slipping beneath the elastic of her bikini. They could hear them laughing.

Marjorie sighed dreamily, 'I'd have loved to have been able to wear a bikini – never had the figure for it – too big in the boobs department.'

Dennis looked across at Marjorie. 'A swimming costume's more flattering – leaves something to the imagination.'

Marjorie returned his look and raised an eyebrow. 'Before disappointment sets in?'

Dennis looked down and said quietly, 'You were never disappointing Marjorie.'

'Oh Dennis! You do remember then?' she said scathingly.

'Of course I remember! I'm not senile, you know!'

They reined themselves in and returned to watching the young couple. The girl was now rubbing suntan lotion onto the man, her fingers moving lightly and sensuously over his body.

'I wonder if people used to look at us like we're watching them – their whole lives ahead of them. They are seriously beautiful aren't they?'

Dennis shrugged. 'I suppose so, if you like that sort of thing. She's too thin – I like a bit of meat on a woman.' He paused for a moment. 'You were a damn fine handsome woman, Marjorie, like an Amazon. I was the envy of the barracks.' And he was. He'd been so proud of her. Their marriage had once been so good, so in tune, when they were just the two of them. What was that saying? 'Three never agree.' Quite a bit of truth in that.

Marjorie smiled. 'I always hated being tall. I would have loved to have been like her, small and petite, vulnerable looking. Everyone thinks I'm so capable.'

'That's because you are, old thing', he said, missing the point.

'Only because I have to be,' she replied wistfully. 'Inside there's a small woman trying to get out.'

Their eyes gravitated back to the young couple.

'How old would you say he was?' Marjorie asked.

'Dunno,' Dennis replied. 'Thirty one – thirty two'

Marjorie nodded. "That's what I thought. Same age as Jamie would have been.'

Dennis remained silent. He pointed to the low stone wall in front of them. 'Extraordinary creatures – lizards – see him? There, talk about camouflage.'

Marjorie turned on him angrily. 'I was talking about Jamie.'

The lizard scuttled away. Dennis frowned and pointed at the empty space. 'Look! You've frightened him off.'

Marjorie leaned across the table. 'You always change the subject when I mention his name – like he doesn't exist.'

'He doesn't,' he snapped back.

Marjorie winced. 'You can be very cruel.'

'Talking about him isn't going to bring him back.'

'I need to keep his memory alive – it's all we have.' She looked so desolate. He knew he was hurting her, but somehow he couldn't stop himself. He was hurting too.

They sat trapped in their own thoughts, neither able to speak. Then Marjorie gathered up her things decisively putting them in her brightly coloured beach bag and stood.

'We can't go on like this... this... silence... it's destroying us – well it's destroying me.'

Dennis looked up at her, trying to find the right words. 'It's not the *silence* that destroyed us Marjorie.'

Marjorie looked away, a pink flush appearing on her neck. She put her hand up to cover it. 'I never blamed you Dennis.' She sounded defensive.

'You didn't have to – it was all there in your eyes.' He said this without rancour.

Marjorie sat back down. 'I was in shock.'

'You called it,' he went on, 'a killing machine.'

'When did I say that?'

'When I showed it to you, the day before his twenty first. You begged me to take it back. You can't have forgotten that."

Of course she had not forgotten. It was in the side shed concealed under a pile of dirty grey dustsheets.

She shook her head silently. 'No,' she said, barely audible.

'You're buying his affection with a *killing* machine – that's what you said.' Those words were etched on his memory and all the other things that had come out at that time. Had he been trying to make a man of him? Yes, if he was honest, he was. Was he jealous of his own flesh and blood? Not really – well maybe – just a little.

Marjorie's voice broke through his thoughts. 'When are we going to stop punishing each other?'

Dennis looked shocked. 'I never punished you.'

'You withdrew your love,' she said. 'I call that punishment.'

'I've never stopped loving you.' He hadn't, but this conversation was going nowhere, opening up old wounds, trying to make each other bleed. If he could put the clock back he would, but he couldn't, and now he had to live with the consequences.

'Let sleeping dogs lie, Marjorie, we get on well enough.'

'Well enough!' She was incensed.

'We share the same interests – we have our bridge, we're passionate about the garden… What we don't do is get in each other's hair like some couples – we don't…'

'Sleep together anymore.' She cut in bitterly.

Dennis took the knotted handkerchief from his head and mopped his brow. "No – well…'

She cut in again, more vehemently this time. 'That's not a marriage, Dennis, that's an arrangement.'

'If it works, why not?'

'I'm sixty-one years old. I'm not prepared to settle for being passionate about my garden!'

Dennis picked up his book and fanned himself. 'Sex is not the be all and end all of one's existence Marjorie.'

'No?' She narrowed her eyes. 'You don't think I believed all those late nights at the golf club, do you?'

Christ almighty, he thought he'd been discreet. 'I don't know what you're talking about,' he finally managed, without conviction.

'Oh Dennis!' she said with humour, 'you need sex as much as I do.'

This was all too much for him. He stood up. 'It's hot, I need a drink… time for a G and T.' He turned and started to walk towards the terrace steps.

'That's right!' she called after him. 'Run away! Turn your back on me which you did when I needed you most.'

He froze on the spot, remembering that awful night. He half turned only to catch sight of the young couple standing on the steps below, their bodies pressed together, their lips devouring each other. Dennis began to lose control. 'I wish they'd go and get on with it – it's disgusting!'

Marjorie was seething. 'It's not disgusting! They're

communicating, Dennis!'

He spun round to face Marjorie. 'Well they don't need to *communicate* in public do they?!'

'We weren't in public you and I. We'd just lost the most precious person in our lives.' She was trying not to cry. 'I needed you so desperately and you... and you...' She couldn't go on.

He had pushed her away, got out of bed and left her alone in the room.

Tears were streaming down her face. He wanted to put his arm around her, hold her close, but instead he gave her his handkerchief and sat back down in his chair.

He looked ahead through the pines to the blissful, calm blue sea. How could he have been so cruel, but how could she have wanted sex. Jamie had barely gone. It was shocking, distasteful and somehow bestial. She revolted him that night.

'It seemed so callous wanting sex,' he said finally.

Marjorie looked at him despairingly. 'It wasn't sex I wanted, it was a oneness I craved... a merging of grief with the only person who understood... felt like I felt but...' she shrugged hopelessly and looked down to the lower terrace.

'They've gone,' she said sadly.

'Who?' Dennis was still distracted.

'The beautiful couple.'

Dennis glanced over the wall. 'So they have, so they have.'

They looked at each other wordlessly.

A harsh discordant sound erupted shattering the silence. Dennis sat up straight. 'What's that?'

The noise came again in short sharp bursts. Marjorie listened. 'It sounds like a motorbike starting up.'

They both turned and looked up to the small car park above the terraces at the side of the hotel.

'I hate that noise, Dennis said vehemently, still looking upwards.

The revving became continuous, a low throbbing growl.

Dennis suddenly sprang to his feet, very agitated and pointed. 'It's that couple... They're not wearing helmets... I better go and tell 'em...' He cast his chair aside and strode purposefully towards the steps.

Marjorie leapt up and followed him. 'Dennis! Dennis you can't – it's none of your business.' She reached out and grabbed his shirt to hold him back. He tried to pull away, his voice urgent. 'But I must before it's too late.'

The revving became louder. Dennis was frantically waving and shouting. 'I say you two, wait a moment... Don't go! Please wait!' He was puce in the face and hysterical trying to raise his voice above the deafening roar. 'Wait – wait!' The motorbike began to move off.

'Stop! Stop!'

It swung out of the car park, the girl clinging to the man, her head resting against his back.

They stood in silence listening to the motorbike receding into the distance up the steep winding hill.

'They couldn't hear me,' he said, his body trembling with released emotion.

Marjorie gently took his arm. 'No darling, they couldn't. Anyway, they would have thought you were quite mad wouldn't they?'

Dennis nodded, allowing her to lead him back to his chair. 'Yes, yes, I suppose they would.'

He sank down into the seat. Marjorie stood behind him, her hands resting lightly on his shoulders. She patted him, about to move away, when he reached up and grasped her hand. She stood still hardly daring to breath.

'Do you know,' she said, her voice a whisper, 'that's the first time you've touched me for eleven years.'

Dennis turned in his seat and put both his arms round her waist. She held his head and drew it in against her chest.

He breathed in the scent of her. 'You have the comfiest breasts in the world.'

'Do I?' Marjorie pulled him in closer, kissing the top of his head.

Dennis sighed, content. He'd forgotten how good she felt.

CASSOCKS *and* KILTS

Before I begin this sorry, or some may say sordid, little tale, I must first apologise for blatantly using you as a form of confessional but I feel, unless I unburden myself now, I shall go completely mad. The story revolves round our greatest friends, Alan and Theresa, in the 25th year of their marriage. Now you may choose to find it all amusing and vaguely titillating or you could treat it as a fable and reflect on your own particular friendships at this time, but I'll let you be the judge of that.

It all started with a phone call, but before I go on I'll give you a few background details first.

Alan and Theresa were the backbone of our little group of friends: the linchpins, the mainstay, the very foundations that we all, without exception, leaned upon. Predictable, reliable, honourable and steadfast are just some of the adjectives I'd use to describe them. They were always there for us in times of crisis and in times of joy.

Alan was a clergyman, a beautiful man both outwardly and inwardly, tactile and demonstrative, with infinite compassion for the frailties of his fellow human beings. So a clergyman should be, you might be thinking, you're right, but how many do you know?

And Theresa, well, frankly, there is only one word to describe Theresa: 'saintly'. There were occasions, and I feel awful saying this, when we could have throttled her. I mean there are times, I think you'll agree, when one should call a spade a spade, but not Theresa, oh dear me no! She found good in everyone and nothing was too much trouble for her. I'll give you an example: when Will, my husband, was laid up with sciatica and I was at that sink or swim stage of my little dress agency business, who stepped into the breech and made Will lunch every day? You've got it – Mother Theresa! Will hated it when I called her that, said I was a bitch. 'Goodness' does have a way of making one feel guilty don't you agree?

There were ten of us in the inner sanctum of our group, including Alan and Theresa. There was Fenny and Mikey. They were the golden oldies and had both long hit fifty. Sadly Fenny had also hit the bottle, but Alan was amazing with her. He became a sort of 'Alan Anonymous', there for her whenever she needed a drink. Poor old Mikey rather resented it; I think it made him feel inadequate. Early retirement hadn't suited him at all.

Noel and Bunty, they're gay men in case you're wondering, and run a terrific florists shop called 'Gay Bouquets'. Now they both willingly would have laid their lives down for Alan, who married them unofficially in his church. Quite something for a C of E parson don't you think? The talk he gave on the day was wonderful: all about love and how, in the eyes of God, all love between two people, whatever their sex, is sacred and should be celebrated not condemned. His voice trembled with emotion; it was a deeply moving experience.

Then there was Scott and Polly. They'd only been in our group for the past ten years but we all adored them. I suppose them being actors made them more interesting than the rest of us. They were great organisers of 'games' evenings. You should have seen Alan playing *Guess Who,* you know that game, when you have to act out a character? His Maggie Thatcher was brilliant and as for his Ann Widdicombe, if you shut your eyes you could have sworn it was her. I think Theresa faintly disapproved though she never showed it, fixed grin throughout while we all just fell about.

And lastly there was us. We'd known them the longest. Will had been at school with Alan and was his best friend. In fact they both studied theology together at Oxford and were inseparable, till Alan took up the cloth and Will went into teaching. Actually, when I first came on the scene I felt that Alan was quite hostile towards me. There's something impenetrable about the bond between two men don't you think? Anyway all's well that ends well. Alan was best man at our wedding. I think it's safe to say that we were their closest friends. After all our kids grew up together, our parents knew their parents and we really had no secrets from each other – or so I thought.

We all live in and around Thatchley Cross. For those of you who don't know it, it's a pretty little market town. Most of the thatched roofs, from which it derived its name, have long since been replaced but it still has an aura of quaint old England. At the time that all this happened we hadn't seen much of Alan who had been away on a sabbatical. Theresa told us in confidence that he'd sort of worn himself out with being a good Christian and was taking time alone to reflect on his own internal life.

Well, now I've filled you in we can go back to the phone call which came late on a Friday night when we were going to bed. It was Alan. He sounded so serious and – well – I think *portentous* is the word I'm looking for. He asked if we could come over the following evening as he had something of the utmost importance to tell us all. I was more than a little hurt;

we hadn't seen him in over three months and he didn't even ask me how I was, so unlike Alan.

Will was his usual switched off self when I tried to talk to him about it. I suppose I should tell you here that ours is not a marriage made in heaven. We never really got the sex thing right and, because we're both quite reserved, the subject has always been taboo. I suspect that I have a low sexual libido and have to admit to being vastly relieved when our Saturday night copulation ceased three years ago.

We all arrived at the same time, each of us bursting with curiosity. Theresa showed us in and was looking absolutely beautiful – in that pure way of hers. I noticed the hall was full of suitcases and briefly wondered why. Alan, who was wearing his cassock, was pouring out wine and handing it to each of us in turn along with a bear-like hug. He looked different somehow: his hair was longer and he had put on weight. We stood around for a bit trying to act as normal. Bunty and Noel were particularly talkative and then Alan walked over to the fireplace and turned to face us all. He cleared his throat and the room fell silent. Theresa glided up and sat serenely by him on the arm of the armchair. I'll try and remember his exact words.

'Firstly I want to thank you all for coming at such short notice,' he said 'and to ask you, my dearest friends, for your forgiveness and for your understanding.'

Bunty said, 'Whatever for?' Typical – he could never keep his mouth shut. We all glared at him.

Alan just ignored him and went on talking and said that what he was about to tell us would soon be public knowledge and probably the source of much derision. The suspense in the room was quite unbearable. Then he dropped the first bombshell.

'This is the last time you will see me wearing my cassock.' He gave us a moment to take that it in. So that was it, I thought, Alan was about to give up God.

Then came the second bombshell. 'This is also the last time you will see me as a *man*.' We all looked at each other, what was he talking about? I looked up at Will who was looking across at Theresa who, believe it or not, was still smiling. Suddenly it struck me she looked just like the *Mona Lisa*, you know that furtive 'I've got a secret' look?

Alan told us that all his life he'd had a problem with his sexuality, 'the mind of a woman trapped in the body of a man.' Those were his words. That from tomorrow we would see him as a *woman*. We must no longer call him Alan but *Alana* and he hoped and prayed that this would not change our feelings of affection for him. We must try to understand that he was putting all *manly* things behind him; I noticed Bunty and Noel nudging each other at that moment.

This may all sound rather fanciful to you but that is exactly how it happened. We all reacted differently. Fenny emptied her tomato juice into a nearby cactus pot, headed straight for the drinks cabinet and poured out the largest scotch I've ever seen. Mikey was shocked to the core; I mean he's a Freemason; he's barely tolerated Noel and Bunty. They, of course, were in their element and went straight up to Alan and flung their arms round him.

Will got up, said he was going to the lavatory.

Scot and Polly just took it in their stride, nothing fazes them – I've noticed it before. I suppose being creative frees the spirit. How much better the world would be if we could all be like them.

Theresa said she would make some tea – amazing woman.

I think the most affected person there that day was me. You see – here comes the confession – Alan was more than just a friend to me. Look, I am old fashioned, I don't believe in all this 'kiss and tell' malarkey but, let it just be said, that 'things' went on between us in the vestry. Call me *kinky* if you like, but men in cassocks turn my low libido on, as do men in kilts. I haven't missed a Highland Games in years and Greek Tragedy is my favourite form of theatre. I also have a predilection for Morris Dancers. We never did the 'full thing', our principles forbade it, but I can state categorically that Alan was a *man* in a big way and, not to labour the point, in full working order. So you can imagine my confusion. I just kept looking up at him standing there in his cassock for the last time; I felt the old familiar excitement in the pit of my stomach and decided I must go home and sort my feelings out.

Will was nowhere to be found, the two vicarage lavatories were empty. I headed to the kitchen to ask Theresa if she had seen him, but she wasn't there – come to think of it we never had that cup of tea. I headed back to the hall where everyone else was leaving. I asked if anyone had seen Will but no one had. There were fond farewells and promises of continued friendship except Mikey who refused point blank to shake Alan's hand. Fenny, who was paralytic, draped herself round Alan, I felt for longer than was necessary, but perhaps I was being over-sensitive. After Alan had closed the front door we went in search of Will and Theresa.

We found the note on the kitchen table leaning up against the teapot. It was Theresa's handwriting but Will had signed his name. It simply stated, no apologies, they were going off to start a new life together. I should have noticed the cases were no longer in the hall. I suppose there were a whole lot of other things I should have noticed too.

Alan and I just stood staring at each other. I found myself questioning my own sexuality. You see here I was facing an unfrocked vicar who was about to wear a frock and, as you don't really know me, I'm going to tell you this: I've never been so excited in all my adult life.

The STUFF *of* DREAMS

Bobby opened her eyes and stared up at the unfamiliar ceiling. It was chilly and the bedroom looked eerie and uninviting in the early morning light. She remembered what day it was and wondered how she was going to survive it. With a weary sigh she swivelled herself out of bed and padded over to the window. She tried to pull the blind up but only succeeded in pulling it down further. Bobby hated all things modern; curtains had character, blinds didn't. She tugged the cord again with irritation and this time the blind shot up with alarming rapidity. Bobby looked out and gasped at what she saw. She stood transfixed, trance-like; this tiny figure of a woman clad in a long white nightdress lost in a world of her own. She smiled wistfully.

Bobby turned round and picked up two bulging stockings hanging from the brass bedpost. She crept up to the sleeping form of her husband.

'Wakey! Wakey!' she said as she playfully bounced one on his head informing him it was Christmas day.

'Can't it start later?' came the gruff reply.

Bobby looked indignant. 'No it can't. It's half past seven. We always open our stockings at half past seven.' It had been a tradition throughout their long marriage even before the children came along.

Jimbo pulled himself on to his elbows and smiled blearily

up at her. 'What's the weather doing?'

'Wet and windy,' she said placing the stocking in his hand.

'White Christmases, the stuff of dreams,' he mused.

Bobby hurried round to her side of the bed clambering in and feeling her stocking in anticipation. Jimbo smiled at her affectionately; she was like an excited child, irrepressible.

'Go on then, start opening,' he said indulgently.

The stockings were full of 'sillies' as they called them, useful bits and bobs. Anything costing more than a fiver had to go around the tree.

Bobby's first present was a plastic ring opener for cans. The arthritis in her hands often left her feeling helpless and frustrated in the kitchen which had become a constant battle with modern packaging.

Jimbo's first present was a flat magnifier to fit inside the map book in the car. Jimbo raised an eyebrow; he did the driving, she did the navigating.

'I'm sure you'll find that very useful,' he said.

The irony was lost on Bobby as she unwrapped a pretty pink floral bath hat. 'Just what I wanted – you are clever Jimbo – it'll match the bath room wall paper.' She perched it on top of her head of thick white hair and turned to look at him.

'Very fetching!' He smiled, pleased that such an insignificant present had given her so much pleasure.

He tore the paper off his next present, a brown woolly hat that resembled a tea cosy. Inwardly his heart sank; he had a drawer full of the wretched things he never wore.

'Don't lose this one,' she said. 'Wear it, it'll keep your dome warm.' She leant out and patted the bald patch on his head.

'Dome indeed!' Jimbo put the hat on and pulled it down over his forehead and squinted at her. Bobby threw back her head and laughed. He'd always been able to make her laugh even through their rough patches of which there had been very few. Bobby ripped the paper off a pair of green and yellow gardening gloves. She held them up and then eyed them suspiciously. 'These look rather *large*, Jimbo!'

'Unisex,' he assured her nonchalantly. 'I got them from the pound shop.'

And so they continued, until Jimbo pulled out a small gold box. Bobby, who was unwrapping a packet of her favourite liquorice All Sorts, suddenly stopped and watched him. Jimbo rattled the box close to his ear. Bobby put her hand on his arm.

'Careful how you open that one Jimbo. It's a special present.'

'We don't do specials in the stockings, Bobby.' He lifted the lid off and peered into the box. He frowned and looked across at Bobby who was suddenly on edge.

'These look like pills, Bobby – blue pills?

'They are,' she nodded. 'Guess what they're for.'

'Constipation?'

Bobby laughed. 'Even I wouldn't give you that as a Christmas present!'

'Indigestion then?'

'No! Silly chump! They're Viagra.'

Jimbo sat bolt upright. His hat rose upwards making him look like a startled gnome. 'Viagra! How on earth did you get hold of them?'

Bobby busied herself with the discarded wrap and said it was a secret. She refused to look at him.

Jimbo wasn't going to let it go. 'You and I don't have secrets, Bobby.' *Little white lies from time to time maybe – but all marriages have those.* Jimbo had a sudden thought. 'You didn't get them from the doctors did you?'

'Of course not!' she replied. 'They wouldn't prescribe them for me.'

'They wouldn't prescribe them for me either,' he blurted out.

Bobby was shocked. 'You never told me that.'

Jimbo looked up at the ceiling. 'Didn't I?' he said, knowing full well he hadn't.

'You never even told me you were going to ask,' she persisted.

'Well I did,' he snapped. He hadn't wanted her to know.

'When?' she said gently.

Jimbo sighed and looked down. 'Shortly after that last abortive attempt.'

He'd heard her crying in the bathroom afterwards when he'd been feigning sleep. Bobby remembered that night only too well. It was August Bank holiday after a lovely day spent walking on the Chiltern Hills followed by supper in the kitchen with a bottle of their favourite red wine and then a game of scrabble which Jimbo, who was a wordsmith, always won. Bobby was an appalling speller and would try to get away with words that didn't exist even in the scrabble dictionary. The evening ended in helpless laughter and a very strong urge to make love, both silently determined that this time it would work. It started out full of promise but ended once more in failure. Jimbo had turned away from her in despair and muttered 'sorry'. There was something so final in that 'sorry'. He'd never turned his back on her before. Yes, Bobby had cried that night; not just for herself but for Jimbo. Sex had been such an integral part of their lives; they never tired of it and never spoke of it either. Jimbo was a man of few words, a proud man. She knew how painful this loss of his masculinity was for him, yet to talk about it would be to admit defeat. Was this the onset of old age? Was this what they had left to look forward to? Decaying body, declining memory, aching limbs, the butt of younger people's jokes, no longer knowing why it was good to be alive? No longer feeling Jimbo deep inside of her? This thought set off another paroxysm of tears and then she pulled herself together for Jimbo's sake. He must not hear her.

They sat side by side, lost in their own thoughts until Bobby said, 'I can't believe Doctor North wouldn't prescribe you Viagra. Why not?'

Doctor North had been on a sabbatical and Jimbo had gone in to see the new *young* doctor with the flashy car and all that hair, who reeked of aftershave, he recalled bitterly. It was for his three monthly check up and he'd casually mentioned that things weren't working too well in the '*nether regions*' and could he possibly have a prescription for some Viagra.

'Oh Jimbo! Bobby burst out laughing. 'Is that how you put it?!!'

'I don't remember exactly how I put it Bobby,' he replied tersely, 'but he got the general gist of what I was saying.'

'What did he say?' she asked.

Jimbo had been trying hard to forget the whole humiliating experience. The young doctor leaning back in his chair smiling at him, having the audacity to ask his age and smiling even more when Jimbo told him he was 73. The doctor had gone on to say that it wasn't unusual at his time of life to experience some erectile dysfunction when trying to have intercourse. He'd then turned away to look at Jimbo's medical notes on the computer while Jimbo waited staring enviously at an erect cactus sitting on the doctor's desk.

Bobby patted his arm impatiently. 'Go on Jimbo, tell me

what he said.'

'He told me,' Jimbo grimaced, 'That I was lucky to be alive, that I survived my major heart attack against all the odds and he personally was not prepared to prescribe Viagra. He then stood up and said, "Let nature take its course, Mr Greenway."'

'What on earth did he mean by that?' Bobby leant over and hugged him.

Jimbo was looking inside the box. 'Why only four pills, Bobby?'

'They're very expensive and er...' *How could she say this tactfully*? 'Well, they might not work.'

Jimbo nodded. 'I see, so it's only once every three months?'

Bobby shook her head. 'Don't be silly. If they work we'll order more.'

Order? Did she say 'order?'

'You still haven't told me how you got them,' he said.

Bobby looked uncomfortable as she picked up her stocking, remarking there were still more presents to open.

'Where Bobby?' His voice was insistent.

'Oh, on the Internet,' she tried to sound casual.

'We don't have an Internet. We don't even have a computer.' He took the stocking out of her hand and brought his face close to hers, his bushy eyebrows knotted together. She would have to tell him the truth.

'Please don't be cross...last week I went out to tea with Nora,' she began, but Jimbo exploded. 'Nora! Oh Bobby! You didn't tell Nora?'

'Not exactly,' Bobby said, remembering meeting up at the tiny teashop, sipping tea out of bone china cups. Nora, her oldest friend, had been transformed: gone was the drab grey permed hair replaced with a chic, highlighted, modern hairdo.

Her normally gaunt drawn face, which gave the impression of austerity, had been enhanced with the aid of make-up, and she looked positively radiant. Nora was sensually devouring a chocolate éclair, cream oozing out of her mouth, with such unashamed enjoyment that it made Bobby feel uncomfortable nibbling away at her arid tea biscuit.

She could contain herself no longer. 'I can't get over how well you're looking, Nora. You've lost years dear…what are you on?'

Nora had arched her exquisitely newly shaped eyebrow and smiled. 'Viagra,' she said.

'Nora's taking Viagra?!' Jimbo sat bolt upright after Bobby recounted the conversation.

'No Jimbo! Harry's taking it.'

'Aah! He's never mentioned it to me, the bugger.' Harry was Jimbo's golfing friend.

'Well he wouldn't, would he?' said Bobby. 'You men are far too proud to talk about your… *private parts*! Particularly when they're out of order.'

'Private parts!' Jimbo scoffed.

'Well it's better than *nether regions*!' she retaliated. 'It took Nora over eighteen months to get Harry to go and talk to Doctor North about it.'

'Really?' Jimbo was feeling brighter already. 'So Harry couldn't… and he was prescribed Viagra.'

'Doctor North told him it was a common complaint and not just older men either.'

Jimbo was lapping this information up, nodding his head and smiling.

Uninhibited now, Bobby went on. 'Trouble is flagging willies are a taboo subject – rather like death.'

'Well they're both so final aren't they?' Jimbo concurred.

'Nothing final about Nora and Harry,' Bobby went on. 'According to Nora, they're at it like rabbits.'

'Like rabbits!' Jimbo couldn't believe what he was hearing.

Nora was prone to exaggerate; Bobby took everything she said with a pinch of salt. 'Well, they do keep going away for what Nora calls "saucy weekends". And they've cut down on booze so they can afford the Viagra.'

That was true. Jimbo had noticed the change in Harry at the golf club. He'd cut out the gin and was only drinking tonic.

'So?' Jimbo said. 'What did you say to Nora?'

'I just said I wished we had some.' She didn't tell Jimbo that she had blurted it all out and told Nora how miserable it was making them both. Anyway, Nora had sworn she wouldn't tell Harry.

'Go on,' said Jimbo.

Bobby continued. 'Nora said why don't I buy a few from her and give it a try?' She looked up at Jimbo to gauge his reaction. He was looking aghast.

'Do you mean every time we want to have sex we're going to have to ask Nora for a pill?'

Bobby hadn't thought that far ahead. She had to think quickly. 'No Jimbo! We'll ask Mark to order them for us on his Internet.'

'We won't! Jimbo erupted. 'I'm not having my son ordering me Viagra! Good God Woman – I do have some pride! We'll get our own computer.'

'Oh yes!' Bobby clapped her hands together gleefully. 'We can go tomorrow, Boxing Day – all the sales start.'

Jimbo was thinking about Harry again. Of late he'd been strutting round the course, not dragging his feet as he'd done in the past panting for his gin and tonic. He wondered if he'd be strutting soon. He looked down at the wonder pills and then across at Bobby. 'Shall I take one now?' he said quietly.

'No Jimbo! I've got to stuff the turkey.'

Of course the family were coming for Christmas lunch. 'Tomorrow then?' he said hopefully.

Bobby beamed back at him. 'Boxing Day, something to look forward to.'

Jimbo chuckled. 'A Boxing day bonk!'

Bobby burst out laughing. 'Oh Jimbo! I love it when you talk dirty.'

Jimbo leaned over and held her shoulders firmly looking deep into her eyes and said, 'Promise me one thing?'

'What?' she said anxiously.

'That you'll wear that charming little hat, it really turns me on.'

Bobby had completely forgotten the bath hat still perched on her head. She laughed and pointed up at his. 'I will but only if you wear yours!'

They both started to laugh as they looked at each other in their silly head gear.

There was a loud knock on the door which startled Bobby out of her reverie where she was standing in front of the window. She turned round confused till she heard her son Mark's voice outside the door asking to come in. He'd brought her tea.

'Come in darling,' she said, going to the door to meet him. Mark entered, tentatively proffering the mug of tea. He was wearing a vivid orange sweatshirt with the word 'Superdad' engraved all over it in black lettering.

'Good heavens!' Bobby said, blinking at it in mock amazement.

Mark grinned. 'Bit bright isn't it? Christmas present from the kids – they bought it with their own money. I thought you could use this.' He handed her the tea. Bobby took it gratefully and walked to the end of the bed.

'Just what the doctor ordered,' she said, sitting down.

Mark was staring at her curiously and said, 'Coming up the stairs just now, I thought I heard you laughing.'

'You did,' she said. 'I was remembering last Christmas.'

Mark came over and sat beside her, putting his arm around her shoulders.

'Oh Mum, this is going to be a terrible day for you. If it weren't for the kids I'd have cancelled Christmas.'

Bobby smiled. 'No, not today. We had such a lovely day together last year. It's tomorrow I'm dreading – the worst day of my life.'

'I know,' Mark said. 'Pam and I thought we'd take you out with the kids.'

Bobby patted his hand. 'No Mark, I shall go home. I need to be on my own with my memories and a large bottle of gin.'

Mark nodded, he understood, 'It was good to hear you laughing just now, you've been so distant and unapproachable somehow.'

'I know,' she said. 'It's been the guilt.'

Mark was taken aback. 'Guilt? What are you talking about?'

'I blamed myself for Daddy's death.'

'Don't be ridiculous! It was a massive heart attack.'

Bobby sipped her tea using the moment to decide whether to tell him or not. *Of course she should.* 'We made love that morning.'

Mark looked away to conceal his surprise. 'So?' he said finally. 'that won't have caused it, surely?' Though he did wonder if perhaps it had.

Bobby went on. 'I gave him some Viagra as a Christmas present.' *Oh my God.* 'Viagra!' he said.

Bobby turned to face him. 'Since Dad's heart problems we haven't been able to... you know... it wouldn't – er...'

'Yeh, yeh, yeh,' Mark said running his hands frantically through his hair, desperate for her to stop. He stood up and walked over to the window saying, 'Hardly surprising at your age. It's quite natural really, Mum.'

Bobby felt incensed by her son's glib presumption that they were past it.

'It wasn't! It wasn't natural at all!' she snapped back. 'Making love was natural to us. When it started to go wrong we didn't know what to do.'

'Well,' Mark said turning round to face her, trying to convince himself as well as reassuring her, 'I'm sure Doctor North wouldn't have prescribed Viagra if he didn't think it was safe.'

'I got them from another source... That was why I felt so guilty.'

'Good God, Mum!' Mark couldn't help himself. 'I wish you hadn't told me that.'

'I haven't told anyone, but inside it's been eating me alive.'

No wonder, he thought but said, 'It was nice that you made love on Dad's last day. I don't suppose many people do.'

'Nice! It was wonderful!' Bobby sighed, remembering Jimbo coming out of the bathroom on Boxing Day morning in his dressing gown. She was still in bed. He was grinning broadly and holding something behind his back. Suddenly he whisked his hand out and hurled her new floral bath hat across the bed to her like a Frisbee.

'We were so happy,' she went on. 'We went off to the sales like a pair of young lovers. We flirted with each other all through lunch in John Lewis.' Bobby giggled. 'We couldn't wait to get home and have another go.'

Why did she need to be so graphic? Mark just nodded his head.

'We felt so alive,' she continued, but then her animated expression changed to one of agony. 'And then that dreaded electrical department heaving with humanity at its worst...' She trailed off as she remembered the bemused young salesman trying to explain to her that no computers come with an internet; that you have to find a provider. She'd turned to look up at Jimbo to see if he'd understood; it was beyond her comprehension. He had been unusually quiet and his pallor was grey with tiny beads of perspiration.

'Are you alright?' she'd said, and twisted back to the salesman. 'It's frightfully hot in here. Can my husband have a chair?' She'd reached out for his hand which was icy cold. Suddenly Jimbo opened his eyes wide and dropped to the floor liked a stone. The next ten minutes were a blur to Bobby. She watched her tender giant of a man sprawled out defenceless on the carpet as one of the customers, who said he was a doctor, tried to resuscitate him and stayed with him till the ambulance men arrived. It was all too late. Jimbo was dead on arrival at the hospital.

Bobby stood up and went across to Mark. 'I don't think he knew what happened, do you?'

Mark was staring out of the window. 'I'm sure he didn't Mum.' He squeezed her hand. 'Do you know it's snowing quite heavily.'

Bobby gazed out. 'A white Christmas, the stuff of dreams.

How Jimbo would have loved that.' Her voice was full of longing.

'Mum you must stop feeling guilty – Dad wouldn't want you to.'

'No I'm not.' She walked across to the dressing table, picked up a framed photograph of Jimbo and smiled at it. 'I'm not feeling guilty any more.'

Mark was taken aback by this apparent change in mood. 'Good, oh good.' he said.

She replaced the photo and looked across at Mark. 'I decided last week the time had come to clear away his clothes – take them down to The British Heart Foundation.'

'You should have asked me to help you,' said Mark, relieved they had now moved on to another topic.

'You know his Noel Coward dressing gown? I thought it might be useful for the local am drams – they're doing *Blithe Spirit* in the Spring.'

Mark nodded enthusiastically. 'Dad always fancied himself in that dressing gown.'

'It needed cleaning,' Bobby went on, 'so I was going through the pockets and I found the box with the Viagra in. I thought I'd better flush them down the loo... Do you know what I discovered?'

Mark shrugged. 'They wouldn't flush,' he suggested.

'No Mark.' She walked over and stood in front of him. 'All *four* pills were there. He hadn't taken one.'

Mark shook his head. 'But you just said...'

'Naturally I assumed he had. I can only think it must have been one last surge of passion.'

She looked across to the window; the snow was still falling. She would never know why he hadn't told her, but one thing she knew for certain: he died a very happy man.

The HONEY POT
A Tale with a Sting

The child stood stock still in the pantry; she could hear the purposeful steps of her Aunt Rosina approaching. This time there was no escape. The honey oozed and glugged its way outwards across the terracotta tiles around the jagged obstacles of broken glass. The door burst open. Claudia's knobbly knees knocked together in unison with the beating of her heart; the tips of her ears glowed pink and warm in the coolness of the tiny room. From the door came a sharp intake of disapproving breath. Claudia kept her eyes glued firmly to the ground.

'Claudia! What have you done?'

Claudia swallowed but remained silent. The air was heavy with ripening cheese. A small black spider appeared jauntily from behind a rack of wine and scuttled over to the honey lake.

'Claudia, will you answer me when I talk to you?!'

'No, don't! Please don't!' the child shrieked, as she watched the spider wade fearlessly into the yellow liquid. 'Stop him!' She brought her hands up to her ears and shrieked again. 'Stop! Stop!'

The legs of the spider twitched helplessly, paralysed in the lethal honey.

'Claudia! How dare you ignore me!'

Claudia crouched down and scooped the spider up with her finger, but it was too late, and lay in a lifeless ball. She began to sob, staring at the rounded sticky corpse.

'He's dead like Papa.'

'No you don't, Claudia, you're not getting round me like that!' The aunt grabbed Claudia's tiny wrist and marched her to the large white sink where she thrust the child's hand under running cold water till the spider toppled off and twirled unceremoniously down the gaping plughole. She then spun her round and placed her hands on Claudia's trembling shoulders.

'Look at me!'

Claudia slowly raised her eyes up past her aunt's heaving bosoms tightly buttoned inside the blackness of her dress, past the solid silver crucifix, into the folds of fleshy chins that nestled on her chest, past down-turned lips and flaring nostrils, finally coming to rest on her aunt's only redeeming feature: large olive green eyes flecked with gold. Papa's eyes had been like that but they reflected life; Aunt Rosina's were cold and unblinking like a fish.

'You've been stealing my honey you naughty little girl.'

'No, I haven't...I was just looking at it and it did fall from my hands.'

'Oh yes? Just jumped out of your hands did it?'

'Yes,' came Claudia's barely audible reply.

'And the three other pots of honey that have disappeared – did they just jump out of the pantry and run away?'

Claudia nodded encouragingly. 'Must have.' Her large brown eyes looked longingly at the door away from her aunt's relentless gaze.

Rosina folded her arms and shook her head despairingly. 'You better go to your room and stay there until you can tell me the truth about the honey.'

'I did,' said Claudia unconvincingly.

'Greedy little girls who eat too much honey grow big and fat and all their teeth fall out.'

Claudia looked up at her aunt defiantly. 'I hate honey and I hate you!' She turned and ran out of the pantry, not stopping till she reached her room at the very top of the house. She threw herself head first on the bed giving vent to her tears once more.

Life changed for Claudia the day her beloved Papa died. Alberto Manzini was larger than life itself, a giant of a man with the voice of an angel, who was following in the footsteps of his beloved hero Pavarotti. Alberto was Italy's fastest rising operatic star. Life was sweet. An apartment in Rome, another in New York and the rambling farmhouse in Tuscany where Claudia and her mother Sofia spent the summer months. Alberto would escape there whenever his hectic schedule allowed him to. He would arrive like a tornado sweeping everything up joyously in his path. His appetites were voracious; wine flowed like an eternal spring, the table groaned under the weight of the food; in the bedroom Sofia moaned with ecstasy under the weight of his body; the maids blushed and flushed in his presence vying for his attention. Claudia was his little princess riding high above his head as he carried her proudly on his shoulders for all the world to see.

The news was brought to them by Alberto's manager Franco. Claudia was on the garden swing when from inside the house she heard her mother's anguished wail; long and haunting like a wounded beast followed by an piercing, angry scream and the words: 'I am going to kill him – bastardo!'

By the time Claudia had reached the house her mother had fainted and there was a flurry of anxious activity all around her. Franco spied the child out of the corner of his eye hovering in the doorway. He hurried across the room and grasped her by the hand leading her out on to the terrace where he gently placed her on his knee. The Tuscan hills were grey and hazy in the distance, the sky harshly blue above them.

'Why is Mama crying?'

'Because, my little one, your Papa has gone to live in God's house.'

Claudia frowned up at him. 'But this is Papa's house Franco.'

Franco thought before he spoke again. 'It was his house bambina, but now Papa has gone to be with God and Mary and Jesus up in heaven – do you understand?'

Claudia's mouth crumpled and her eyes welled up with tears. Heaven and hell happened to people when they died. 'Why has Papa had to go to heaven – can't he come back?'

Franco looked away from the child's imploring face. He spoke as if to himself. 'Papa's spirit was too big for this life, it just burst out and drifted away – so, no darling, he can't come back.'

The days following the dreadful news were fraught. Sofia was inconsolable, her moods swinging from heart-rending grief to uncontrollable anger. Photographs of Alberto were ripped from their frames and shredded into tiny pieces. The magnificent oil painting of him above the fireplace standing centre stage at La Scala, Milan, his arms outstretched to an adoring public, had been defaced with glutinous dollops of spaghetti. Claudia, who was only six, found all this hard to understand.

The funeral was in Rome: a grand but sombre affair attended by the paparazzi and celebrities from all around the world.

Claudia stood gripping her mother's hand in a sea of black watching Papa's coffin as it was reverently lowered inch by inch into the freshly dug grave. The strain showed on the faces of the grim looking pallbearers in the intense heat of the mid-day sun. Suddenly the grip from her mother's hand tightened as a vision in a bright red suit appeared. She had platinum blond hair topped by a red pillbox hat and carried a single red rose in her hand. A tall black man in a white designer suit walked at her side holding a red and white polka dot parasol to protect her from the sun. The crowd of mourners parted to let them in. She looked across at Sofia and Claudia, inclined her head and then gently brought the rose up to her lips, kissed it, stepped forward and released it on to the descending coffin. There were gasps of surprise, murmurs of disapproval, uncomfortable looks and flash bulbs flashing. The vision in red turned and walked away from the mourners without a backwards glance.

It was at the wake that Claudia discovered how her Papa had really died; tired and bored with being ignored, she crept away upstairs and went into a small bedroom to lie down, but the bed was a mountain of coats and cloaks. She crawled underneath it lying on the floor sucking her thumb and sniffing her comfort rag. She was about to fall asleep when two women attired in black came into the room to collect their jackets. They talked about the service, complained about the lack of food and commented on the unsuitable amount of make-up Sofia was wearing. Then one of them said in lowered tones, 'Well, she must have very mixed feelings about him after…you know?'

'Actually, I don't know,' the other woman replied, and then added conspiratorially, 'all I know is there is something to know and nobody cares to tell me.'

'Well don't say I told you,' the other replied in even lower tones, 'but our dear Alberto was…now, how shall I put this delicately? He was right in the middle of…Well, he had his finger in the honey pot – so to speak…'

'You don't mean,' the other enunciated the words with relish, '*in flagrante delicto*?'

'Exactly! Going at it like a young bull – his heart couldn't take the strain. Rumour has it they had to prise them apart in the ambulance.'

The other woman clucked with disgust and glee and then said disparagingly, 'Men! They're all the same where *honey* is concerned – poison – I'm glad I don't have it any more!'

Claudia rolled on to her back in the little attic room and stared up at the ceiling. Below her aunt was calling her to come down and say she was sorry. She longed to go back home where it was safe, but Mama was resting her nerves in a special place. She prayed that her aunt would not find the other pots of honey she had thrown down the well. She thought of lovely cuddly Papa eating the poison honey and said out loud, 'Don't worry, Papa, I'm going to make all the honey in the world go away – I promise you.'

YESTERDAY'S CHILD
A Monologue

It was January, Thursday the thirteenth to be precise. I remember writing in my diary later that it should have been a Friday. I was quite superstitious in those days. That night I was on top of the world. I had been to my Weight Watchers evening and lost three pounds – everyone had clapped and made a fuss of me and I was the centre of attention; a unique experience for me. I hated weight-watchers at first – it was Rob who kept nagging me to go. He said I didn't get out enough so I went to please him. I was quite shy then and didn't make friends easily, but they all seemed to like me there, nobody looked down on you. Anyway, I drove home looking forward to telling Rob about the evening. He was a wonderful listener; actually he was a much better listener than he was a talker. The dark, silent type, you know – you were never quite sure what was going on inside his head... and obviously I didn't.

I let myself in, calling out, 'Home James!' Daddy's stock phrase which I always used and always made Rob laugh. He would call back, 'Come on in, James!' Silly really these rituals, but we all have them don't we? That night he didn't. The lights were all on so I called again – thought he was probably in the loo – still nothing. I wasn't worried, I mean why would I have been? I'd only seen him two hours before and he'd spent the day at home fixing up all the things in the house that needed repairing. He'd even walked me down the garden path and kissed me 'goodbye' at the gate quite passionately, which surprised me. I remember looking round to see if any of the neighbours were watching, to be honest I hoped they were, but it was dark and all the curtains were drawn. He smelt nice. He didn't usually wear aftershave unless we were going out. He said, 'You take care now, Prudence.' Normally he would say, 'Drive carefully.' It wasn't till later that I thought about that...and he always called me 'Pru' never 'Prudence'. I hated my real name. It was Mother's idea of a joke. I was a *surprise* baby – actually *shock* is a more appropriate word. Mother had my brother and my sister by the time she was thirty; I arrived seven years later. Mother had wanted to abort me, but Daddy wouldn't let her. So she called me Prudence as a warning to herself to be more *prudent*. I used to tell that story to make people laugh, but I never found it funny.

He was nowhere in the house. The loft hatch was closed – Rob had his den up there. I suffer from vertigo so had never seen it. I even checked the garden shed. He appeared to have eaten the shepherd's pie I had taken out of the freezer for him so I decided he must have been called out on an emergency, though usually he would leave a note. Rob was a plumber and not just any old plumber; he was brilliant, too brilliant for his own good. He was called out at all hours of the day and night. I begged him to turn his mobile phone off after News at Ten. I would argue with him that people could surely wait till the morning. He just smiled and continued to sleep with it under his pillow. There was one woman who always seemed to get a blocked loo in the middle of the night; Lord knows what she put down it! She was foreign, Spanish, with a name that sounded like 'Consolation'. She had a husky voice and was usually in tears. Rob was a big softy when it came to tears – except for mine. I said to him,

'Rob, why on earth don't you give that foreign woman a new lavatory?' He said he had but it was all to do with the antique plumbing in her mansion block.

Mother never knew he was a plumber; I told her he was a heating engineer (Daddy's idea). Not that I was ashamed or anything, but Mother was an unrepentant snob. Lucky for Rob he had a Scottish accent; you can't really tell what class people are with a regional accent, though Mother did ask me once if he was from the Gorbals. Actually Rob never talked much about his background, always changed the subject. I had to tweak things out of him over the years. When we first started going out I called him 'Mystery Man', but that was what made him so alluring.

I found Rob through the Yellow Pages. We had a blocked drain at work and my boss told me to find a plumber so I opened up the plumbing page, stabbed it with my Parker pen and hit Robert McClusky. When he walked in half an hour later my legs turned to jelly. He was like a film star – imagine Antonio Banderas with a dash of Daniel Craig thrown in and, *voila,* you have Rob. Only difference: Rob was incredibly short and wore high platform shoes to elevate himself. I made him endless cups of tea that day and, just before he left, he leaned over my desk and said, 'What time do you finish tonight?' I thought he was just being polite and went into a long rigmarole about my hours. He then said something like, 'You wouldn't fancy a drink, would you?' His accent is quite strong and I got the wrong end of the stick, jumped up and said, 'Of course, tea or coffee?' It didn't occur to me that someone so gorgeous could be asking me out. Well, I still saw myself in those days as a bit of a 'dumpling', Mother's childhood nickname for me. Daddy used to call me 'Podge', which wasn't much better, but somehow he made it sound affectionate. Poor Mother, she couldn't help it really. I was a blot on her landscape. Not that I was hideous or anything, but she was so glamorous and bewitching, everything about her was on a grand scale: her mouth was wide and generous with a perfect set of dazzling white teeth. She was tall with wonderful bosoms; they used to heave whenever she was worked up about something. Men couldn't take their eyes off them, even Rob. It's the only thing I've inherited from her – only mine never seemed to heave.

I went outside to the front of the house to check if his van was there, and then remembered it had gone in for a service, so I came back in none the wiser and made myself a cup of low fat cocoa. I tried him on his mobile, though he used to get very cross if I rang him when he was on a job, and said I should understand that if he is lying under a bath or got his hand round somebody's u-bend, it's not very easy to answer, or hygienic. Rob knew how obsessive I was about cleanliness. The answering service was on, so I left a message telling him off in a jokey sort of way. Actually, deep down I was quite annoyed – no other plumber would work the hours he did. He would not be told though; he would go into a strop if I ticked him off, and then refuse to talk to me for days on end. I was a bit like Daddy was with Mother, 'peace at any price' – it's easier. I had a soak in the bath and at ten- thirty was sitting up in bed writing my diary. I've always kept one ever since I was sent to boarding school at the age of eight. This was a happy entry, the last one for a long time: full of my day with Rob and that lingering kiss he'd given me at the gate. I still wasn't too worried that he hadn't rung, and decided he was probably just being considerate; usually I was asleep by ten o'clock. I dropped off with the light on and the next thing I knew it was 6-30 in the morning when I was woken up by the sound of wailing sirens and cars racing down our road. I turned over to see if Rob was awake, but his side of the bed was untouched. Perhaps he'd slept downstairs or in the spare room. But no, he hadn't come home. I didn't know what to do, who to ring. Rob was a one-man band; if a job was too big for him he did not take it on. 'Never rely on anyone Pru,' he used to say to me. 'Then no one can let you down.' He was totally independent – a loner.

Of course I immediately thought the worst – accident – run over by a car, a heart attack – he was forty-eight... or a brain haemorrhage. The butcher dropped dead from one a few weeks before, in front of all his customers, and he was only forty-two. I began to cry. I thought of my Rob lying unclaimed in a morgue while I lay sleeping in bed, and then I pulled myself together. He would have had his wallet with him, all his cards are in it, he would easily be identified and someone would have rung me. 'Calm down!' I said to myself, make yourself a cup of tea and think this through. I broke my New Year's resolution, piled the sugar in; sweet things have always been a comfort to me. I was sitting at the kitchen table sipping my tea when I remembered something, something very important: Rob was wearing his tracksuit when he said goodbye. That must have meant he was about to go jogging; he jogged for hours on end sometimes. My heart began to pound. We'd had loads of vicious muggings in our area, there were police notices everywhere warning people to be vigilant. I knew exactly where he ran; down our road, up another and on to the Common... it was also a short cut to the station but Rob wouldn't let me use it, said it was too dangerous for a woman on her own. I felt sick. Probably he had been stabbed and was still lying there unnoticed in the bushes. No one would have seen him in the dark... I used to beg him not to run on the Common at night. 'If it's dangerous for me,' I said, 'then it's dangerous for you too.' He laughed at me. 'Stop being a worry-guts, Pru, I can take care of myself.' He thought he was invincible, saw himself as a big man, but actually he was barely five foot two. I was eight inches taller than him; that's why I could never wear high heel shoes and I stooped to make myself smaller.

I flew upstairs, flung on my tracksuit and trainers, grabbed my raincoat, as it was pouring with rain, and then dashed out of the house. I ran down the road, must have been around seven o'clock. It always surprises me how many people are up and about at that hour in the morning bustling off to work. Nobody took any notice of me pounding along the pavement but that's London for you – Martians could land and nobody would notice, all too busy. By the time I reached the Common I had a terrible stitch. I wasn't used to running. Rob said I was lazy; he bought me an exercise bike for my birthday but he was the only one that used it. It's ruined the look of our dining room. I begged him to keep it in the shed but he said, 'No one uses the dining room, Pru.' Which was true. We had never gone in for dinner parties because of Rob's unsocial hours. It was a shame really because I was a good cook. Mother was hopeless in the kitchen; it was all those years living in India surrounded by servants that ruined it for her. So I learned from a very early age that the one way I could please her and earn her praise was by cooking the evening meal. I used to spend all my pocket money on cookery books. The more exotic the dish the more lavish the praise.

There were two empty police cars parked in the road. I headed up towards the Common, through this wooded part, a minefield of dog poo. I hated that woody part; it seemed to attract men in dingy raincoats. We'd been warned about them...

I've never understood flashing. Once, when I was about eight, at one of Mother and Daddy's roulette evenings at home, I was sitting in the bath, fortunately for me a bubble bath, when the door opened and in walks Major Patterson, this ex army friend of my parents. He said, 'Hello my dear, wondered where you'd got to.' I had handed round the olives and cheesy bits at the beginning of the evening. He'd been really nice to me and kept patting me on my head. He sounded so normal and jolly that I said 'hello' back and slid down quickly under the bubbles. He then closed the door and I thought, *phew he's gone* – but no! The next thing I knew he was standing by the side of the bath smiling and unbuttoning his flies. Then he took his thingamabob out and showed it to me – I'd never seen one before – it was quite revolting. I just stared at it and then I said, 'Please can you put that away?' and he said, 'Of course, my dear.' Which he did, then patted me on the head again, wished me 'good-night' and went out of the bathroom.

Later, when I told Mother, she went white with rage and slapped me across the mouth – it made my split lip bleed. I was always picking my lips, the groove was so deep it even bled when I smiled. 'You naughty girl,' she said. 'You're telling lies again! Major Patterson is very high up at the Ministry of Defense.' And as far as she was concerned that was the end of it. That night my diary was full of the injustice of grown ups with graphic details of Major Paterson's horrible 'thingamabob.' My diary was my best friend; I could tell it anything without fear of recrimination.

I came out of the wooded bit to the top of a slope which leads down on to the open part of the Common. It was teeming with rain, water was trickling down inside the collar of my raincoat.

I stopped to survey the Common, but I wasn't wearing my

contact lenses; I'd forgotten to put them in, so it took a moment to adjust my eyes and realise that the area was crawling with police; it seemed like hundreds of them. A large part was being cordoned off just by the derelict café. An ambulance was driving away. There were police cars everywhere with whirling blue lights. I could feel the tension in the air even from where I was standing. My heart began to leap all over the place. I tried to swallow, but all the juices in my mouth had run dry. Though I knew something awful might have happened to Rob, I was still hoping that I was wrong. Everyone does that: think up the worst scenarios so they won't materialise – a sort of fail-safe mechanism. I stood there like a drowning rat, unable to move, too terrified to go over and find out what had happened in case…

'Excuse me, madam,' a man's voice said.

I nearly jumped out of my skin. I hadn't realised anyone was there. I turned round and came face to face with a balding man in a raincoat who was emerging from a clump of trees behind me – *Oh God no! What a time to be flashed* ! The funny thing is…well, not *funny* exactly, peculiar more like, that I suddenly asserted myself; I was so highly charged with emotion, about to find out I was a widow, that I wasn't going to allow some horrid pervert to sully the occasion. I shouted, 'Go away!' I'd wanted to say the 'f' word, but swearing never came naturally to me. I tried to when I was younger, but it always sounded false and made me blush. Mother swore like a trooper; she relished bad words.

He looked at me like I was a mad woman. He wore tiny little round-wired spectacles. He reached inside his raincoat and said, 'Let me show you my…'

Suddenly I saw red. 'Don't you dare get it out or I'll kick you in the goolies!' There! I said it! 'Now, bugger off!' Mother would have been proud of me. Rob would have been shocked out of his mind; he was very old-fashioned as far as women were concerned.

The man held up a card and said, 'Detective Inspector Cooper. Sorry if I frightened you Madam.' I wasn't falling for that, and anyway I couldn't see. He could be showing me a bus pass for all I knew.

I remember when I was six and we were living in Knightsbridge, Mother used to go to Harrods to have her hair done. She'd let me wait for her in the pet shop on the fourth floor. I used to stand in front of the cages gazing longingly at all the puppies. I was at that age when sweet things overwhelmed me. I would spend exactly fifty-five minutes in the pet shop and would then head off down all the escalators to the ground floor and meet Mother at the entrance to the food halls.

Anyway, on this particular day I arrived down at the food halls entrance and went to sit on the bench facing the escalator so I could see Mother when she came down. It was midday, Mother's hair do was always at eleven. The sale was on and it was very busy. I must have waited for nearly half an hour and was getting bored, so I decided to go and see if I could find her in the hair salon at the top of the store. Another excuse to go on the escalators again which I adored doing having got over my initial fear of them. I was just stepping off about halfway up when I felt this heavy hand clamp down on my shoulder. It gave me a fright. I turned round and looked up at this tall, lanky man wearing a brown felt hat. I'd seen him downstairs leaning against a wall reading a newspaper and I thought I'd seen him looking at me over the top of it just as I was about to pick my nose.

'And where do you think you're going to young lady?' He had thin lips and looked very stern.

'I'm going to find my Mummy, I said.

'Oh no you're not! I'm the store detective and you're coming with me.'

'Why? I'm not doing anything wrong.' I was trying to be brave, but inside I was really scared.

'We don't allow children to go unaccompanied on the escalator.'

He then grabbed my arm and dragged me across to the other escalator going down.

'I want Mummy.' I was trying not to cry and he was hurting my arm.

'She'll find you in our room for lost children,' he said. If I'd been older I might have realised that rooms like that did not exist. I remembered the *lost boys* in *Peter Pan* who were taken away from their parents. It didn't occur to me to resist him; I was a child who obeyed commands. He stood close behind me on the escalator pressing me up against him, both hands clasping my shoulders. He smelt of chips and had long fingernails. They were jagged and dirty. I began to feel queasy. Suddenly, I heard Mother's voice shouting my name. I looked around and saw her moving upwards on the other escalator waving frantically at me with a huge green and gold carrier bag in her hand. She looked different: her hair was shorter, though her white streak was just the same. It curved away in an arc on one side of her face; she had had it ever since she was a child. It was the shock of hearing her father shoot himself when he lost all his money in the depression.

I waved back and shouted. 'The man's taking me to the lost children's room!'

'What! Stay where you are, Prudence!' Her voice startled everyone; it was her imperious tone that she used when she wanted to be obeyed. There was a dramatic hush. 'That's an order, Prudence!'

It's difficult to stay where you are on a moving escalator. I looked up at the man.

'That's my Mummy,' I said, 'can I go now?' He was muttering under his breath. I thought for a minute he was going to strangle me and then he let go, sweeping me to the side and hurtled down the escalator shoving people out of his way. One woman began to scream. Mother was shouting at me to wait for her on the next landing. It caused quite a hoo- ha. The police were called in but they never caught him. It's funny to think I might have been a 'News Headline.' That was all to come.

The bald 'so-called' detective was speaking to me.

'I must advise you to leave the Common. This is no place for a woman to be out on her own.' Certainly it wasn't and he was coming closer; I wasn't going to stick around.

I started to run away down the slope, calling over my shoulder, 'I'm reporting you to the police!' I kept glancing back at him as I ran, but he didn't follow, just stood there bold as brass shaking his head.

Suddenly he waved and shouted, 'Look out!' Crash! I hadn't seen Marjorie Miller jogging across my path. Luckily for me she's an enormous woman, so it was rather like colliding with an air bag. We both keeled over and rolled down the slope together. Marjorie had been 'slimmer of the month' for the last three months at Weight Watchers. She must have been at least twenty stone – so much easier to lose weight when you're that big. I used to like standing next to her in our exercise class as it made me feel relatively slim beside her. I really liked Marge, she was very down to earth – came from Buxton and had one of those soothing Northern accents. Anyway, we sat for a moment in stunned silence both splattered in mud. Marjorie's face was bright pink and matched the colour of her kagoul. Then I couldn't stop apologising. I told her I'd been running away from some pervert in a mac. I pointed up to where he was but of course he had gone. She was most concerned and looked quite ferocious. I think she would have tackled him herself if he'd still been there.

'You ought to tell the police,' she said. 'There's enough of 'em here – I don't know why they don't spread themselves out more. I mean he's not going to be hiding right by the body is he?'

'What body?' I said. My heart was in my mouth.

'Oh didn't you know? A woman's been murdered... bludgeoned to death. Two boys found her body half hidden under a bush this morning on the way to the station.'

'How do you know?' I said.

'I spoke to one of the detectives. He told me. Said I shouldn't be running on the Common till they found him. "Sod that for a lark," I said. Nobody's going to stop me jogging – but you did!'

We both laughed and then I burst into tears. She was really sweet, put her arms round me. Of course she thought I was crying for the murdered woman – it was such a relief to know my Rob was still alive.

Marjorie walked back home with me; she only lived two doors away... even offered to come in and have a cup of tea. I said, 'Better not.' I don't know why. I needed someone to talk to, but I was still hoping that Rob had turned up while I was out and would be there with a rational explanation. So I'm afraid I lied to her; I told her Rob had been working late and was still asleep. Little did I know the trouble that lie was going to get me into.

There was a postcard from my best friend Judy lying on the doormat, and two letters for Rob. I could hear the answer phone bleeping from the sitting room. I rushed in and switched it on, praying it might be Rob and holding my breath it wasn't some hospital telling me he was ill, but it was neither; the caller didn't leave a message. I did wonder who could be ringing me at 7.30 in the morning – probably blooming *Spanish Consolation* with another frigging blockage. You could see the mood I was in.

Later, after I'd changed into dry things, I sat in the kitchen reading Judy's postcard. Our friendship began at boarding school. She was terribly homesick and I befriended her. We were called 'Little and Large' by the other girls; she was tiny and rather delicate. Judy was knapsacking her way round Australia, finding herself again, having at last walked out on her violent husband and given up her job as a book editor for a well known publisher. She used to take refuge with us from time to time. Once Rob was so incensed by her husband's behaviour that he offered to 'beat the living daylights' out of him. I remember I was rather shocked. It was a side of Rob I had never seen before. Judy, tactful as ever, declined sweetly. She was the only person I could have talked to.

I was craving for something sweet. I kept thinking of the Belgian chocolate ice cream in the freezer, Rob's favourite. What the hell, who diets in a time of crisis? I went over to the freezer, opened the door and there was Rob's shepherd's pie, uneaten, sitting on the top shelf. I peered at it and saw that there was some writing etched out in the mash. I carried it over to the light. It said '*SORRY*'. I kept staring at it. Did he write 'sorry' because he didn't want to eat it, or because he'd been called out and *couldn't* eat it... I then had a dreadful thought: was Rob about to kill himself, was this his suicide note to me? No, he'd write a proper one surely, not in a shepherd's pie? Anyway, why would Rob want to kill himself? We were happy together in our own funny way – eight years in February. My favourite wedding photo was on the pine dresser in the kitchen. I'm smiling out towards the camera and Rob is looking at me like he'd won the crown jewels. I did look radiant that day.

It was only a small wedding, in a church, just family: my family and a few friends. We could have had a great big do; it was either that or a deposit on a house. Rob chose the house. Mother called him a tight fisted Scotsman. Well, it was more sensible really... I mean Rob had no family. His mother gave him up for adoption when he was born. You couldn't really blame her. She was only sixteen when she became pregnant with Rob after a one-night stand with a Spanish waiter on the Costa Brava. Rob's adopted parents were killed in motorway pile up when he was three. He had a terrible childhood, in and out of institutions and various foster parents who always sent him back. Poor Rob. I found it hard to imagine him as a wild boy, but he was always in trouble. It wasn't till he was sent to a reform school in the Outer Hebrides, and came under the wing of Brigadier Kilpatrick, that he began to change. 'The Brig', as Rob used to call him, was his mentor. He could be terrifying, Rob said, but also incredibly kind, and really cared for all the boys. It was he who encouraged Rob to learn a trade. 'A good plumber is like pure gold Laddie, you take my word for it.' And Rob did. The Brig came to our wedding wearing a very splendid kilt. Rob introduced him as friend. It wasn't till after we were married that he told me about the reform school; probably worried I'd go off him. It may seem funny, but Rob put me on a sort of pedestal, treated me like royalty. Nobody had ever done that before.

When I first met Rob I was a bit hung up about sex. I think Mother put me off it. She was always talking about it – to be honest I think she and Dad were always doing it. I used to sleep with a pillow over my head so I couldn't hear all the jungle noises they used to make. She told me the facts of life when I was five, and I so didn't want to know. Even the way she ate would make me blush sometimes... especially corn on the cob. She was a very sexual woman, my Mother, it just came naturally to her. Sometimes I think I never quite got the hang of it. It's all to do with rhythm, isn't it? I mean I could not dance to save my life...Rob was a brilliant dancer – he never missed his Spanish dancing class on a Friday night, not even for plumbing!

I'd only had sex once before I met Rob. I didn't tell him though, didn't want him to lose interest in me, so I elaborated on my relationship with Jean Pierre. Jean Pierre took my virginity in the Bois du Bologne, under a rug which smelt of Camembert cheese. He never asked me out again. The whole experience was deeply painful in every way.

Why didn't I ring the police to report Rob's disappearance? It was that *'Sorry'* in the shepherd's pie that stopped me. I had to find out more for myself. I went back upstairs to investigate his wardrobe: no change there. The clean shirts and jeans I'd put away a few nights before were exactly where I'd hung them. In fact, his whole wardrobe was looking exceptionally pristine, the result of a massive clear out over a recent bank holiday, when he'd taken at least three black bags of clothes to Oxfam. Not before time. Rob rarely threw things away. The only thing missing was his *Olé kit,* the suit and special shoes we'd bought in Barcelona for his Spanish dancing class. But he often left those in the van in case there wasn't time to come home and change. The van! I rushed downstairs to ring the garage where it was in for its service. But just as I picked up the receiver I became aware of a man peering in at me through the sitting room window. I yelled with fright and dropped the receiver. It was the man in the raincoat – the flasher – he must have followed me. He ducked away. *Oh God* I thought, *I must ring the police.* The doorbell rang – I suddenly needed to go to the lavatory – I have an emotional bowel. According to Mother I was potty trained by the age of one. I hung on and dialed 999, but while it was ringing a police car drew up outside the house. Relief. I rushed upstairs, threw open our bedroom window to call out, but saw two policemen getting out of the car and talking to the man in the mac who was pointing up at the house. They all saw me at the same time and beckoned me to come down. Of course he *was* a detective. Detective Inspector Cooper! I felt really silly. I should have apologised but how do you say, 'I'm sorry but I thought you were a perv.' I just glared at him. We were standing in our hallway. I thought they might be coming to tell me some news of Rob, but instead he asked to speak to him.

'He's not here, he's gone to work.' I wasn't about to tell this man that my husband had disappeared.

'Oh?' he said. 'Your neighbour said he was catching up on some sleep.'

Bloody Marjorie! 'He was.' I had to think on my feet. 'He had an emergency call out, he's a plumber.'

Cooper smiled at me. 'Ah, I suppose he went in his camper van, did he?'

Camper van – I had to laugh. 'I'd hardly call our battered old van a camper van… no, it's gone in for a service, he'll have gone on his bike.' Actually Rob didn't have one. Why did I say that?

He then told me that someone reported a camper van illegally parked on the Common late last night. They'd checked the registration number and Rob's name and address came up.

'Well.' I said, 'I'm afraid I can't help you …we certainly don't own a camper. I wouldn't be caught dead in one! You must have been given the wrong information.'

Cooper then asked me where Rob had gone.

Why didn't I shut up, why didn't I just say, 'I don't know'? Instead I said, 'A Spanish woman, she calls him out at all hours of the day and night.'

Immediately they all looked interested, and Cooper asked if I knew her name.

'It sounds like *Consolation*.' I then attempted a joke. 'My husband calls her "*a pain in the anal canal*". Silence. 'On account of her blocked system.' Nobody laughed.

D.I. Cooper flipped open a notebook and glanced at it. 'That wouldn't be Consuela Hickson?'

'No, I don't think so.' I was lying. I'd seen that name in Rob's customer file. 'Why?' I asked.

Cooper looked straight at me. 'Her body was found on the Common this morning.'

Whoosh! I ran into the downstairs lavatory and emptied out the entire contents of my stomach. They were still there when I came out. Everyone looked uncomfortable – well it is impossible to have an upset stomach quietly. They told me to get Rob to ring them as soon as he returned. D.I. Cooper gave me his card.

I couldn't face work so I rang St Osmund's Primary. I was the school secretary. I told them I had an upset stomach – no lie there!

Then I rang the garage and spoke to Freddy the service manager; he'd looked after Rob's vans for years. He was very friendly. 'Hello Mrs. McClusky, still 'ere then? Thought you'd have taken off by now!"

'Off?' I said.

'In your new camper van – nice innit?'

I was speechless. It was so completely unexpected. I should have found out more of course, but I just said, "No not yet...oh, excuse me Freddy, there's someone at the door,' and hung up. I felt numb. Why would Rob buy a camper van without telling me? And what was he doing parked on the Common late at night? What was I going to say to the police when they found out everything I'd said had been a lie? They couldn't suspect my Rob of murdering Consolation surely? I made a mental note to stop calling her that, it wasn't funny any more.

I resorted to my usual source of comfort and took out the Belgian ice cream.

It must be obvious to anyone reading this that Rob had left me. I knew he had been depressed for quite some time. Actually, to be precise, since Daddy died seven months before. After Mother's death Rob and Daddy grew very close, particularly towards the end, when Daddy had become extremely absent minded. To be honest I think it was the drink. Rob did everything for him, nothing was too much trouble. Daddy was on these very strong adrenal steroid hormones, had been for years – Addison's disease. Rob would pop in every day, morning and night, to make sure he took them. I remember feeling slightly usurped at the time, but then I figured that Daddy was really a man's man and would much prefer Rob's company to me fussing around him trying to make him eat and cutting him back on his shots of whiskey. In fact it was Rob who discovered him on the morning that he was dying and went with him in the ambulance to the hospital. I remember Daddy's last words to us. Rob and I were sitting either side of the bed, each holding one of his hands. He opened one eye and said, 'Sorry – well you can't take it with you, can you?' He smiled and then slipped into a coma. He certainly didn't take it with him, his estate was bankrupt! My parents had been borrowing on the house by Richmond Park for years to finance their lavish lifestyle. The receivers took everything. The only thing we inherited were the extortionate solicitor's fees for sorting out the sorry mess. Rob was more disappointed than me; we were going to buy a flat on the Costa Brava. He had this dream of one day finding his father. He was almost fluent in Spanish, always listening to his tapes even when he went jogging.

I'd nearly finished the tub of Belgian ice-cream when I had a moment of clarity: Rob was having a mid-life crisis and had taken himself off to the Costa Brava in search of his Dad. He hadn't told me because he knew I would have tried to stop him as, firstly, we could not afford it and, secondly, I would have told him that no man is going to remember or own up to a one night stand they had 45 years before! But then my theory collapsed. What was that camper doing on the Common? And how did he buy it?

I sat painting glass all morning. It was my passion. Actually, I was rather good at it, and it transported me out of myself, allowed me to daydream. I did it in our spare room. Rob had built me lots of shelves where I displayed all my favourite pieces. This room was going to be for our child...but 'my childbearing hips', as Mother used to call them, never fulfilled their purpose. Two miscarriages – a lot of tears... there was a time when I would have to cross the road if I saw a pram coming towards me. I do enjoy the children at our school.

I found myself thinking about Mother, I often do. She died two years before Daddy. Lung cancer. After she was diagnosed she refused all treatment, just doubled her intake of nicotine. I still have a vivid picture of her sitting up in bed applying her bright red lipstick in-between puffs on a Marlborough Ciggie, as she called them, saying, 'Thank God I haven't got to face old age!' She went two days before her seventy-fifth birthday. The last time I saw her we had a dreadful row. We were on our own. Daddy had gone to fix her evening Campari soda. She said out of the blue, 'How's the "Little Scotsman"?' I hated the way she referred to Rob as 'little'. 'Not making you very happy in the bedroom department, is he?'

I stood up. 'How dare you say that!' She had hit a raw nerve; Rob rarely made love to me, he was always too tired.

'He has bedroom eyes – I wouldn't trust him further than I could throw him,' she said blowing out a cloud of cancerous smoke. That was it. I stormed over to the door shouting over my shoulder, 'There is more to life than sex, Mother!'

'What?' she said. 'My poor old Prune, you're wilting before you ever bloomed.'

I left the room without a backward glance. The next time I saw her she was in her coffin. Even dead she looked more glamorous than me.

The police arrived on my doorstep at six o clock the following morning to arrest Rob. I just burst into tears; I couldn't believe this was happening. I allowed them to search the house before agreeing to go to the police station with them to 'help with their enquiry.' I felt the eyes of Linden Avenue staring at me as I was driven off.

I was questioned for nearly six hours. They did bring me some tea and toast. The lies I had told really got me into deep water and it took a lot to convince them that I really did not know where Rob was. They even listened in a bemused way to my theory on him having a mid-life crisis. The trouble was the evidence was piling up against him and the longer he stayed away the guiltier he looked. They had proof that Rob had bought the camper with cash – £25.000, the exact amount drawn out of Consuela's account the day before – and traded in his van. There was CCTV footage of Rob going in and out of her block of flats at all hours of the day and night. They informed me they had found Rob's tool box in a cupboard at the flat with his Corgi Registration certificate inside.

I explained to them about her faulty plumbing, but D.I. Cooper said, 'Mrs McClusky, we're talking a luxury penthouse here. There's a maintenance man on permanent call out. He said her plumbing was faultless.' That really hurt. Not just the implication of what he was saying, but the way he looked at me when he said her plumbing was faultless. And why was Rob's tool box at the flat? He took it everywhere. They then brought up a photograph on their computer of a blue and red zip up suit bag and asked me if I recognised it.

'It's a wardrobe bag,' I said, 'Why should I recognise it?'

'Look carefully in the left hand corner madam,' D I Cooper said.

They magnified the corner and I could clearly see the initials **RM** stitched in red. Of course I recognised it, I'd stitched them on.

'Yes,' I said. 'It looks like the bag my husband carries his Spanish dancing clothes in.'

There was this sort of frisson in the room before Cooper looked me in the eyes and said, 'The body of Consuela Hickson was found zipped up inside that bag on the Common early yesterday morning.'

I needed the lavatory – like immediately – they did let me go but things got no better when I returned. Forensic evidence showed that Consuela had been bludgeoned to death in her apartment before her body was taken and dumped on the Common.

'Someone would have seen her being carried out of the apartment, surely?' I said.

Cooper said, 'Not if the perpetrator used the service lift at the back of the building, which goes down to the car park.'

Why was he telling me all this stuff – he didn't think I'd done it, did he?... Mind you, I did have a motive. The camper van had been parked near the service lift since 10 a.m. on Wednesday morning, and Rob was seen entering the apartment block at precisely 11.25 on the Thursday night. The night porter had seen the camper leaving the car park just after midnight thirty seven minutes later.

'I don't know what you want me to say,' I said. 'I just know Rob could never kill anyone.' Cooper then raised his voice. 'Then tell us where he is, Mrs McClusky.'

'I don't know,' I cried out, and burst into hysterical tears.

It was the main story on the news. Not only was Consuela an ex-beauty queen from Rio de Janeiro, but she was married to someone known as *'Ronnie the Rat'* Hickson, a notorious drugs baron who was serving a ten-year prison sentence. She had recently filed a divorce suit against him. I couldn't get away from the wretched creature staring out at me from the telly. I had to admit she was beautiful – in that small Latin way.

On Sunday I decided to go and buy the newspapers and see what they were saying. As I stepped outside flashbulbs went off. For one blissful moment I thought I was being shot. Death would have been one way out of it. It was the press, quite a few of them, taking photos and shouting questions at me. I slunk back inside and slammed the door.

I rang Marjorie Miller who was really sweet on the phone. I asked her if she'd buy me some Sunday papers. 'Oh love,' she said, 'you don't want to upset yourself with those!' She had obviously read them all and five minutes later handed them over to me in our back alleyway. Rob was plastered on the front pages of all the tabloids, wearing his *olé kit* dancing with Consuela. So that was where he must have met her. *The Sun's* headline was *The Dancing Plumber and his Spanish Moll.* It seems that members of his dancing class were more than helpful to the press with photographs and snippets of gossip about their love affair. Rob did look gorgeous, his neat little bottom moulded inside those shiny black trousers. Pathetic, I was still in love with him.

The next few days were a blur. I did make a point of looking smart and doing my hair and make-up before I left the house. It's funny but at school when I entered the staff room they all stopped talking. I can't explain it, but they looked at me in a different way. For the first time in my life I had become a conversation stopper.

The letter from Rob arrived at the end of the week. He'd sent it to the school. Sensible really, I'm sure the police were intercepting our mail and I knew the house was being watched. There was always somebody sitting in a car outside gazing into the middle distance.

I recognised Rob's handwriting immediately, it's spidery and slopes backwards; needless to say Mother was the first to remark on that. I took it into the lavatory to read.

'Dearest Pru,' is how it started. 'I'm sorry for all the pain I've caused you. Please believe me when I tell you that everything you've read and heard is a tissue of lies.' Oh I did so want to believe him. He told me that he had been framed by *'Ronnie the Rat'.* Consuela had received threatening calls telling her to call off the divorce or face the consequences. Rob had agreed in a weak moment to help her get out of the country and go to Zurich, where there were secret funds stashed away in a safety deposit box. I tried not to think *where* that weak moment might have been, though he did assure me their relationship was strictly platonic – they were lovers on the dance floor only, rather like Torville and Dean were on the ice. I could hear Mother scoffing from her grave! Consuela had offered to pay him a large sum of money, but she had bought his silence too. Hence just the *Sorry* on the shepherd's pie. He even explained the late night phone calls and nocturnal visits to her flat to attend to her so-called 'plumbing.' 'She was terrified Pru,' he wrote. 'She kept hearing noises in the night and thought she was about to be murdered in her bed.' That had a sort of logic for me, and would explain the hysterical crying on the phone. He was going to tell me the whole truth on his return and planned to surprise me with the camper, which he was allowed to keep as part of his payment. Together we would travel the world, just the two of us. His explanation rang true for me, perhaps because I wanted it to. After all, I told myself, he hadn't taken anything with him other than his Spanish kit had he? I did suddenly remember the three black bags he said he was taking to Oxfam but I pushed that thought away.

Rob went to collect her late on the Thursday night. She didn't answer the door so he let himself in using the key she kept hidden in the aspidistra pot on the landing.

She wasn't there, but had left the camper keys with a note written on toilet paper on the hall table. It said he must drive the camper to the Common near the derelict cafe and meet her there. She'd explain later. He flushed the note down the toilet as instructed. He said he should have smelt Ronnie the Rat there and then. Consuela would have phoned him had she been delayed. They must have forced her to write the note before they killed her. He was being set up and he'd flushed his only proof away.

He drove the camper to the Common and sat waiting for over an hour. He realised that something had gone badly wrong. He was cold and went to the wardrobe to fetch his fleece. He pulled open the door and his clothes bag fell straight out. He half unzipped it and saw Consuela's stiffened body. He panicked, carried it out of the camper and dumped her under a bush covering her with shrubs and leaves. He caught a train that night but said it was better for me not to know his destination.

I believed him – about the murder I mean – even felt sorry for Poor Consolation, sorry, Consuela. I could afford now to be magnanimous. She wasn't a rival anymore. Rob told me how much he loved me and asked me to wait for him. He was going underground for a while, not just from the police, but from Ronnie and his henchmen, who would be out to kill him. I did wonder why.

Three days later I got my answer. Three more packages arrived at the school from Rob: one with a key, the other with an address of a bank in Zurich and a code number for a deposit box. The third packet contained a map and instructions telling me exactly what I had to do, and on no account to take the key home, but hide it at the school and wait till I heard from him. Consuela had entrusted Rob with the key as she knew Ronnie's gang would be instructed to look for it after she had absconded from the flat. It was kept hidden in a wall safe. Consuela replaced it with a fake key to buy them a little time.

Rob was caught hiding in the back of a Spanish container lorry after a routine inspection by customs officers at Calais docks. He was brought back to London and Wormwood Scrubs to await trial. Bail had been refused. Not only had he run away but also the evidence against him had become more and more incriminating. A wrench had been found hidden in a laundry basket in a bathroom in Consuela's flat; it was covered in Rob's fingerprints and traces of Consuela's blood.

When I went to visit Rob in jail he wept he was so pleased to see me. He looked diminished without his platform shoes and the full beard didn't suit him. The time of death had now been established. Consuela's gold ring watch she wore on her middle finger had been smashed at the time of the attack. She must have put her hands up to protect her head from the blows. The watch had stopped at five past six. Rob's defense lawyer was cock-a-hoop; Rob had been home on the Wednesday evening seeing me off to my Weight-Watchers class. It was such a relief to know that he was innocent and that I could be his saviour. They had asked for other witnesses to come forward but no one had seen us at the gate. I gave my statement to the police.

It was a strange time waiting for the trial, which, after two preliminary hearings, was fixed for May 31st. I remained in my job; we needed the money. I placed the key in a sandwich bag along with the code number and details of the bank. I dug a very deep hole in the rockery in our back garden and hid it there, filling it up with earth and placing a large stone on top. It was against Rob's wishes, but I did not want the school implicated in any way.

I visited Rob whenever I was allowed, and was as deeply in love with him as when our relationship started out. He flirted with me again and the things he said turned me on. I fantasised every night about his homecoming and how we would make love: on the kitchen table, the stairs, in the bathroom. My passion knew no bounds. I began to write erotic love stories and found it deeply therapeutic. It also passed the time. That was how I survived my boarding school days, writing imaginary stories about the staff and some of the more spiteful girls. I could articulate in writing what I could never convey in speech. Judy, who was the only person allowed to read them, was enraptured. On paper I felt sexy, funny and fearless. In life I was a wimp.

As the trial drew nearer Rob became anxious about me being alone in the house; he said that one of these days Ronnie would discover that the key to his deposit box had been swapped. His henchmen would leave no stone unturned to find it. I didn't dare tell Rob where it was hidden. He was also worried that I might be on their hit list as the only witness for the defense. I agreed to go away until the trial. I needed a break and a bit of country air. So I invited myself to stay with my sister and brother in law in the Dordogne in France.

I had a horrible time. They did nothing but pour vitriol on Rob. Said he'd only married me for my money.

'What money?' I said.

'The money he thought Daddy was going to leave you.'

Priscilla's tongue was more acidic than our Mother's. The weather was awful, with monsoon-like rain. I stayed in my room writing furiously on the new laptop I'd purchased before my trip.

I couldn't wait to come home away from all the sniping and innuendos. They didn't even wish us good luck for the trial. I arrived at the house early in the evening. I could not believe what confronted me when I opened the front door; the whole place had been ransacked, every drawer had been tipped out, our books ripped apart, the cushions slashed open. There were feathers everywhere, I began to sneeze violently.

Nothing had been spared, even the contents of the freezer. The kitchen floor was a sludgy lake of liquid and food. I shut the door on it and crept upstairs.

All my precious glass had been smashed to smithereens. Rob's clothes had been cut into tiny pieces and scattered along the landing. I walked into our bedroom and stood ankle deep in feathers staring at the gutted mattress and my duvet. I rushed out into the garden but the rockery had been untouched, not a stone upturned.

I was numb with shock. I suppose that was how I was able to climb the loft ladder and go into Rob's den for the very first time.

It was a sea of paper and rubbish. Empty black bags everywhere, the contents tipped in piles that had been rifled through all over the wooden floor. Rob's Spanish dancing mat was in the middle of the room. I remember hearing his little feet pounding away through the ceiling to the strains of Ravel's *Bolero.*

I suddenly became aware of masses of little white pills strewn all over the mat – odd; Rob wouldn't even take a painkiller. They looked like Daddy's steroids, until I saw lying nearby seven or eight empty Hermasita tins; that was odd too – Rob only took sugar. I started prodding about in the piles of upturned rubbish. In one I found full bottles of Daddy's steroids and crumpled up pieces of paper, mostly computer print-outs; I took them under the naked light bulb to see more clearly. They were all on Addison's disease and the steroid medication prescribed: its effects and risks. Small sections had been highlighted – the words are still imprinted on my brain – *'Too rapid a reduction of steroids could lead to adrenal insufficiency, low blood pressure and death.'* And another one: *'Never skip doses for the condition because life threatening reactions may occur.'* I sat motionless, staring into space, and then – **Wham!** It hit me like a bomb exploding in my head. My husband had killed my father; everything fell into place. He'd withdrawn Daddy's steroids and replaced them with Hermasitas; the pills looked identical. My blood ran cold. All that love I had invested in him suddenly crashed and I finally grew up, no longer yesterday's child.

I never went back to the house. I booked into a small hotel under another name. The insurance paid up and five months later I sold it. Fortunately the mortgage was in my name.

In the witness box at the trial Rob's defense barrister questioned me about Rob's whereabouts on the day of the murder. I said I could no longer remember so could not testify under oath. My initial statement to the police was then read out in court and I was asked why I had made the statement if I could not remember. I looked down and did not answer.

The judge finally said, 'Well Mrs. McClusky? We're waiting.'

'I was frightened,' I muttered.

The judge's voice reverberated around the courtroom. 'Speak up, Mrs McClusky, the jury can't hear you, and neither can I.'

I looked straight at Rob. 'Because I was frightened of what my husband might do – I know he's capable of murder.' My voice broke and I dissolved into tears. There was a deathly hush in the courtroom.

Rob leapt to his feet shouting at me.

'You're a lying bitch! She's lying, she's bloody lying!'

The judge threatened to exclude Rob from the proceedings if there was another outburst. I was dismissed as an unreliable witness who had told a tissue of lies when first interviewed by the police. The defense barrister in his summing up speech suggested that I had lied out of vengeance, and advised the jury to forget what they had just heard in the witness box.

'Hell hath no fury like a woman scorned,' he said dramatically. He then turned to the jury. 'Why?' he said. 'Why would my client kill the woman he loved, the woman he intended to marry when his own marriage was dissolved? I have seen the papers he filed for divorce with his solicitors a week before the death of Consuela Hickson. Remember ladies and gentlemen of the jury, it is not my client's morals that are on trial here today.'

This revelation left me cold; nothing could hurt me any more. I was devoid of all feeling.

Rob's defense that he had been set up by the criminal fraternity could not be substantiated. The time on the watch, the prosecution had pointed out, could have easily been changed by the perpetrator to give a false lead – a well-known ploy. Perhaps that's why Rob had kissed me at the gate, to establish himself not at the scene of the crime. But the plan had misfired.

Rob was found guilty and sentenced to life. I didn't look at him when they led him out of court, nor did I feel guilty. I still don't know to this day if Rob had killed Consuela, though logic tells me he had no motive, but I do know he had as good as murdered Daddy so, in my book, it was rough justice.

The next few years I would describe as my years in the wilderness. I needed to get away, not only from the long–reaching arm of Ronnie the Rat and his mob, but from myself. I had to leave Prudence behind and re-invent myself. I decided to disappear for a while and flew to join my friend Judy, who was then in America still on her journey of self-discovery. I hadn't realised there was so much to find and what fun it was. We were the perfect match for each other, both recovering from marital trauma. Judy had never found me dull and so I blossomed in her company. We had enough money – me having taken redundancy from the school and the healthy profits from the house. We really did see the world. I changed my name in every port of call. We sampled the customs, culture, food, drink, music and the dance. I became sexually alive, as though waking up from a long sleep, and discovered I did have rhythm after all. I was suddenly free and intoxicated with life. I also began to write again – and everywhere we stayed inspired in me a different story. Judy would then edit them. She was critical, but always encouraging, and eventually sent one off to a competition in America. To my amazement, not Judy's, it won. She had become my mentor and seen in me what no one else had seen before. I did have a talent which needed careful nurturing, and so all those former suppressed feelings exploded on to paper and I could not stop writing, but I needed somewhere to settle down so I could write a novel. We moved to Italy and rented a house in the Tuscan Hills.

My first novel has been a runaway success, with the film rights already optioned, all thanks to Judy who touted it round London and landed me a three-book deal. Judy tells me I have changed beyond recognition: my hair, which is cropped short, turned white soon after the shocking discovery in Rob's den. I have finally accepted my height and grown into it with pride. I even flaunt my bosoms. When I occasionally look in the mirror, a handsome statuesque woman smiles back at me. I am becoming famous, but have to remain anonymous. Judy is my spokesperson and manager, who would guard me with her life like a small fierce terrier. Rob is still in jail but Ronnie the Rat is due to be released any day now, and no doubt will soon start looking for me. This worries Judy far more than me; I tell her Prudence McClusky no longer exists. The key and all the other stuff, as far as I know, are still buried under the rockery in our old garden. I often used to speculate as to what was in that box in Zurich. What if Rob had been lying to me? What if it was something other than money, something lethal, something dangerous, and that's how the idea was born for my best seller.

It is called 'The Lethal Key' **by Venus A. Wakes** – my nom de plume – chosen by Judy, which my publisher adores.

And now, four years on, here I sit on the terrace of our newly acquired house beside a lake. I am jotting down these memories of my life when I was just plain Pru, with strict instructions to Judy not to publish them till after my death.

Judy has just brought me my evening Campari soda. It makes me think of Mother. I can feel her approval beaming down on me – I raise my glass in salute.

Her plump old prune is positively blooming!

The LAMBETH WALK

Ralf scowled into the fire. He had never felt so humiliated in his life. He sat firmly on his bottom trying to conceal the dampness. The smell of the disinfectant permeated his nostrils making him feel bilious. Today every last vestige of his male dignity had been stripped away from him.

*How **dare** she and who in the name of dog **was** she? And **why** had she brought him here? He was happy where he was. Alright so 'happy' is perhaps too strong a word but when you're on your last legs you don't expect 'happiness'. Two square meals a day and somewhere to sleep is all you ask for.*

Ralf dolefully surveyed the vast room; the windows at either end were both securely locked; the light outside was turning into night. The floor was covered in a pale blue turf-like substance that made him sneeze and deadened out the familiar noise of feet.

Oh for the pungent smell of Arthur's feet.

Ralf returned his gaze to the fire as pictures in his mind came flooding back. Arthur's rasping voice calling, 'Grub's up, mate!' They'd sit together in silent familiarity, Arthur chewing arduously and Ralf trying to control his natural tendency to gobble. When they'd finished eating they would stretch out beside the fire and snooze. How Ralf had loved that little fire. The popping noise it made when Arthur turned it on, its white bones turning to a warm glowing orange except for one cracked bone that gave a light relief of blue.

Ralf stared at the ornate grate in front of him. Round black stones and dancing flames that never changed their pattern and gave out no heat at all. A solid slab of cold white marble patterned with swirls of smudgy grey surrounded the fireplace; it put Ralf in mind of the cemetery he and Arthur used to visit. Standing there side by side, heads bowed, sometimes Arthur wiping a tear from his eye. 'Funny old life Ralf. We're born so we can die, can't make head nor tail of it.'

Ralf stood up and turned his backside to the fire. He raised his eyes then stared in disbelief.

*Now I've seen everything! How did **they** get up there?*

Brightly coloured fish were swimming in the wall, plunging and surfacing, skimming through greenery, their mouths opening and closing in helpless O-like glugs. Spirals of bubbles gurgled upwards. A fat golden fish, its eyes squinting through the glass, stared obliquely back. Ralf shuddered and turned away from their silent scream for help.

They're trapped but what can I do? I'm a prisoner just like them.

He sat down again and thought about his captor: a large woman with wide swaying hips and an expanse of wild frizzy brown hair and even wilder eyes. She spoke in a funny voice which he found hard to understand. But then he'd never been a one for females – yes, they had their uses but he was too old for all that nonsense now; companionship was all he craved and Arthur had been the perfect companion.

He remembered with longing their daily walk to work. Stopping halfway across Lambeth Bridge with its balustrade of black, gold and orange. Arthur leaning over the top, Ralf's head resting on one of the soft curves lower down.

'They can keep their Taj Mahals, Ralf, you won't find nothink to compare with that.'

They would both stare out intently, Ralf not quite sure what he was supposed to be staring at, but none-the-less enjoying being included in Arthur's random thoughts.

'That there stands for stableness Ralf, that there is where all them politicians go to work of a morning.'

He'd reach inside the breast pocket of his shabby coat and withdraw a large round watch on a blackened silver chain. He'd squint his eyes into the distance then look down at the watch in his hand.

'Good little timekeeper this, Ralf,' he'd say, replacing it in his pocket. 'Keeps up with its big brother over there.'

They'd continue their walk over the bridge and then down the concrete steps that led off it into a small park separated from the river by a thick stone wall. Sometimes, when Arthur's breathing troubled him, they'd stop and rest a while on one of the benches. Arthur would take out a rusty tin from his side pocket, open it and, with yellow fingers, deftly roll a piece of white paper tightly round little brown bits of strong smelling grass. He'd glue it together with spit and thumb before putting it in his mouth and lighting it with a tiny pink tipped stick. It would flare briefly and Arthur would suck in noisily before blowing out a cloud of smoke that made Ralf's eyes water. As the thin white tube in Arthur's mouth diminished so he would start to cough: a rasping, searing, gut-churning cough that rattled up from deep inside of him. The people round about discreetly moved away; even the fat and fearless pigeons scattered to a safer distance. Ralf would edge in closer allowing Arthur to feel the warmth of his body nestling up beside him. When the coughing ceased they would set off again, past the great buildings, through all the hordes of people, stopping to look at the giant-sized statue of a man supporting himself on a stick. Ralf likened the expression on his face to that of a fierce-looking bulldog.

'We won't see the likes of him again, God rest his soul,' Arthur would wheeze, raising two fingers in a gesture of salute before crossing the busy road and heading on up Whitehall. The last part of the journey was arduous, uphill towards 'the Circus' as Arthur used to call it. He would stop from time to time to catch his breath until at last they reached the wooden booth into which Arthur would disappear, leaving Ralf outside to wait. Minutes later he would reappear, his head emerging from the middle of a square white board in front of him and another on his back. The boards were covered with scrawly black writing. Thus clad the two of them would slowly walk to and fro between the Circus and Leicester Square. People would stop and encircle them peering at Arthur's middle or his back, sometimes putting on their glasses, sometimes asking questions, most of them incomprehensible.

'Is this Li-ces-ter Square?' was a common one, and one that Arthur understood. But others floored him. 'Isn't *Cats* showing any more?' Ralf's hair would stand on end. *Cats* – he hated them!

'You got me there,' Arthur would reply scratching the back of his head.

Ralf would walk two paces to the side of Arthur, his eyes ever watchful and protective, his heart fairly bursting with pride.

Ralf's ears pricked up. He could hear her voice outside the room punctuated by shrieks of metallic sounding laughter. He stood up and, with one eye warily fixed on the closed door, began to edge his way to the other end of the room. Something sharp brushed up against his leg. He looked down and froze.

Good Dog – what's that?!!

He was staring into the open mouth of a giant sized cat, its fang-like teeth bared and snarling, its amber eyes ablaze. Ralf's hair stood up on end as he closed his eyes and prepared to meet certain death. When nothing happened he opened them again and saw with horror that the skin of the animal lay flattened out and lifeless on the blue floor beneath it.

All right so nobody – well nobody with any sense – likes cats but. this is going too far.

He gingerly stepped away from the lifeless form, his attention caught by a glass-fronted cabinet. His spirits lifted, for it was filled with beautiful birds perched on branches.

Ralf and Arthur loved birds and every morning in the winter months Arthur would pull the newspaper out of the broken window pane and slip his fingers through sprinkling crumbs all along the ledge. Silently they would watch them swooping down from the adjoining rooftops, crowding onto the narrow space, their heads darting back and forth, vying with each other for the meagre offerings. Their favourite and the friendliest was 'The Red Red Robin' as Arthur used to call him.

Ralf stepped closer to the cabinet and pressed his nose up against the glass.

My Dog, I was just thinking of you!

A robin redbreast was foremost on the branch. He'd never seen his feathered friends so still, their little eyes startled and fixed. Ralf nudged the glass willing them to move though deep down he knew that the life had flown from these birds and that they were stilled forever in a glass prison on a rootless tree. Ralf felt sick; he now finally understood why this horrid woman had brought him here.

I'm going to be snuffed, then stuffed and stuck on a wall!

Ralf's heart pounded against his chest as the door opened and his captor entered. She was talking to herself, a small black object tucked under her chin.

'She's never forgiven us, thinks we lost him deliberately – so I just hope it's going to work. I don't know what we'll do if it doesn't. I'm no dog lover and Quentin's allergic to them!' This last remark she found hugely amusing and threw back her head laughing. 'Quite – killing isn't it!' Ralf's legs turned to jelly.

'He's an ugly old mutt too!'

*I'm a **dog**, Lady, or hadn't you noticed?*

'Still we might get away with it,' she peered across at Ralf. 'He's very like him – even smells the same!' This produced another burst of insane laughter. 'Anyway, better go, they'll be here in a minute... yah, I'll keep you posted, bye.'

She strode across the room towards Ralf, who retreated beneath a chair.

'What's the matter with you silly old thing?'

***Old** yes - **silly** I'm not!*

She crouched down on the floor beside him, craning her neck forward, her face parallel with his. She reeked of flowers. Ralf drew back his lips and, with yellow teeth, snarled.

She flinched away, 'Oh no you don't!'

Oh yes I do!

'They told me you were harmless, so you'd better stop that or I'll take you back.'

Ralf set up such a paroxysm of snarling that he nearly choked himself.

'Good God, Prudence, what's going on?' It was a man's voice. The woman stood up. 'I didn't hear you arrive – where's your Mother?'

'She's sitting in the car, won't get out. Says she just wants to go home. The hospital staff pleaded with her to stay. She's refused any more chemo, won't take painkillers, says she'd rather have whisky. Can you talk some sense to her?'

The woman sighed. 'Well you see if you can do something with **him**. I think our plan's misfired. We'll have to take him back to Battersea Dogs home.'

Her feet disappeared to be replaced by a lank lock of grey hair which flopped downwards. Followed by the upside down, thin white face of a serious looking man. He looked piercingly at Ralf through gold-rimmed spectacles then nodded approvingly.

'You'll do – very like – yes indeedy!'

What will I do? What's he talking about?

Suddenly the man's face contorted as he let out an enormous sneeze showering Ralf's coat with spray. His spectacles shot onto Ralf's paw which he cautiously tried to retrieve without success as Ralf renewed his snarling with increased vigour. The head vanished. Ralf lightly gripped the spectacles with his teeth and flipped them out beyond the chair. The man's hand snatched them up.

'Well – thank **you!**'

*Don't mention it! At least **he's** got manners!*

Arthur had manners; always said 'please', always said 'thank you' even when he was dying.

Ralf's mind drifted back to their last day together. It was bitterly cold on the walk to work; round every corner the wind assaulted them like a mugger with a knife leaving Arthur breathless and blue.

'Shouldn't 'ave come out today Ralf boy, should we? These

boards don't 'alf weigh a ton.' He kept stopping and stamping up and down.

'Can't feel me feet, they've gone all numb.'

Ralf padded over and sat down on Arthur's worn-out brogues trying to warm him up. A gust of wind seared across the square. Arthur's boards rattled. He reached inside his pocket for his watch, trying to hold it steady in his shaking hand, his old eyes straining in the fading autumn light.

'Let's go 'ome Ralf, can't take no more of this today.'

Suddenly Arthur staggered backwards and then lurched forward weaving like a drunkard before clattering to the ground; the board on his back juddered to a standstill. The watch skidded away down the sloping pavement. A small crowd of disapproving onlookers began to gather looking sideways on as if this in some way disassociated them. Ralf ran round in desperate circles appealing with his eyes for help. A large boot quickly covered the watch but Ralf sprang over, snarling and snapping. He pounced on the offending boot which tried to shake him off but Ralf persisted and retrieved the watch carrying it over to Arthur and dropping it gently in the old man's hand. Arthur's eyes fluttered open, his fingers closed over the watch, his voice barely audible.

'Thanks, mate, good little timekeeper this.' His breaths became shallower and fainter with long pauses in between and then the last silent breath.

The rest was all a blur: a wailing noise, blue flashing lights, Arthur being carried off and shut away inside a large white van which then drove off; the crowd dispersing, isolated voices.

'What's going on?'

'Some old tramp just kicked the bucket.'

'Oh,' said one disappointed voice. 'We thought something

exciting must have happened.'

Ralf stood unseen, wishing the great Dog above would take him too.

He wandered for days on end homeless and hungry finally collapsing on Lambeth Bridge. Here he too was picked up and placed inside a van with a snooty looking poodle who refused to look at him.

There were raised voices outside the room again.

'I'm sorry, Kathleen.' It was the woman's voice. 'We thought, just while it was growing, we didn't mean to offend you.'

'I came into the world bald and I shall die bald.' The voice was haughty and authoritative. 'Now please go and eat. I'll wait in the drawing room till one of you can take me home.'

'You really should have something to eat, Mother, you need to build your strength…'

'What for?'

'I give up!' The man let out an exaggerated sigh.

The door opened and closed again. The room was silent. Curious, Ralf emerged from his safe retreat and looked around. It was dark outside and the lighting in the room was subdued. He moved stealthily towards the door planning to make his escape the next time it opened. He sat down to wait but gradually became aware of a human shape sitting bolt upright and motionless in a chair, the firelight showing up the whiteness of her face in stark contrast to the darkness of the room, her head devoid of hair. Ralf wondered for a moment if she too was stuffed. He crept a little closer to observe. A brown square box rested in her lap.

'Who's that?' she said turning her head. 'Come here at once, stop lurking!'

Ralf felt compelled to obey and crept guiltily out from

behind the sofa.

'Come **here**!' she commanded. 'You're all a blur.'

Ralf went meekly over and stood in front of her. Her smell was familiar: fusty and strangely comforting. She reached out and cupped him under his muzzle with her bony hand. She scrutinised his face. No one had looked at him like that before. Finally she spoke.

'I knew you'd come back Ben, I wouldn't let them tell me anything else.' She smiled a smile of such infinite love that Ralf had to resist the temptation to give her a smacking great lick. Instead he just stared back.

'Don't you recognise me, Ben?' Her eyes were pale blue and watery. In a sudden movement she touched her bald head. 'No, of course you don't.' She looked down at the box in her lap, removed the lid and took out a clump of silver grey hair. She stood up and proceeded to place the hair on top of her head, adjusting it while she inspected herself in the gilded mirror above the fireplace. 'We shall be going home in a short while.' She turned. 'There! Now do you know your mistress?' She looked quite human and, after all, 'Ben' wasn't a bad name.

I can answer to that. Anything to get out of here!

They heard voices outside the room. She snatched the hair from her head, rammed it back in the box and firmly secured the lid. The door opened and the man came in followed by the woman.

'Why are you sitting in the half dark Mother?' the man said switching on a light.

'We are quite happy Quentin,' she replied.

'We?' said the frizzy-haired woman.

'Yes Prudence *we*. Ben's come back, I always knew he would. We're waiting to go home.' She reached out and touched

Ralf's head reassuringly. The man and woman exchanged triumphant looks.

Ralf felt the old strength return to his legs. He straightened up and took his place beside his saviour. He was on guard once more.

ORPHAN ANNIE

'No – you – can't – get – a – man – with – a – gun!' Sandra belted out in full voice landing on one knee, her arms outstretched, her smile radiant and expectant only to be greeted with, not applause, but two loud bangs on the adjoining wall of the flat next door.

'No you can't – and I'll bloody shoot you myself if you don't belt up!' Came the voice of her neighbour, Ian Bishop, a normally polite man whom she thought was still away. She'd been practising the routine for at least two hours, enough to try the patience of a saint. She'd buy him a bottle of wine tomorrow by way of an apology, if she got the job.

If – the story of my life, she thought, slumping down into an armchair. 'I could be famous *if* – *if...* what the hell! She surveyed her cosy little flat affectionately, its walls cluttered with theatrical memorabilia and tried not to think about her mortgage which had fallen into arrears or the, as yet, unopened letter from the building society standing on the mantelpiece.

Sandy Downs, as she was known in the business, had somehow always missed the boat. No one who knew her doubted her talent; she could sing, she could dance, she could act. Indeed, when she was married to Jack Johnson, better known as 'Jack the Lad', more famous for his philandering than his acting ability, she was always considered the talented one with a glittering future ahead of her. However, a nervous breakdown following the suicide of her mother, while she and Jack were touring in Australia, changed everything. For two years she couldn't work and then Jack packed his bags and left her for several other ladies but not before squandering the legacy her mother had bequeathed her. He then went on to become a household name in television soap.

Sandy wasn't bitter but the years of disappointment were beginning to show in her once vivacious and attractive face. She was 38-years-old and realised that her days of being a juvenile were numbered; she spent more time in front of a computer these days than an audience trying to earn a living. Tomorrow was the first glimmer of hope after nine months out of work. Almost enough time to have had a baby... *if* she had a man... she'd probably missed the boat there too.

At least they've asked to see me this time, she told herself. It was the title role in *Annie Get Your Gun*, a part she had played fifteen years before to great critical acclaim. This was a twenty-six week contract on the number one touring circuit with a strong possibility of a short run in the West End over the Christmas period. The production was already ten days into rehearsal time when disaster had struck. Jeannie Stewart, who had been playing Annie, injured her spine in a car accident and had to be replaced.

Sandy's Agent, Sam, had sounded confident when he rang to tell her about the audition.

'The odds are in your favour, sweetheart, you've even got the same measurements as Jeannie and they've made half her costumes.' This, Sandy knew, was a distinct advantage; she was barely five foot tall and wafer thin.

'Orphan Annie' her mother used to call her. Sandy's stomach still knotted when she thought of Mo. The driving force of her early life, her rock, her anchor, who held them together when Dadso, an artist, lost the will to paint and drank himself into oblivion and early death. Sandy was eleven when he died. Mo had managed, despite all the difficulties and the relentless struggle to make ends meet, to give her a childhood that was magical and fun. She was a wonderful mimic and could make Sandy laugh till her sides ached. Mo was her confidante, her mentor, her protector and, when Sandy launched her career, she was her greatest fan.

But then there had been the darker side; the side that Sandy didn't know, the side that made Mo take her life without any explanation.

Sandy abruptly pushed herself out of the armchair. It was time for bed.

Next morning Sandy sat on the tube clutching a large carrier bag in which she'd put her cowgirl costume, hat and boots. She'd hired them the day before from a theatrical costumier, an expense she could ill afford but justified if it helped her land the part. She felt nervous but buoyant; she knew today was going to be special. She'd had one of those unexpectedly symbolic dreams in which her mother had appeared.

They were walking and talking, arms linked, in a deep forest dappled with sunlight giving the effect of intricately woven lace upon the ground. Sandy could smell her familiar scent of sandalwood as they walked; Mo with the same lopsided gait, a legacy from childhood polio. The same infectious laugh, head thrown back her curly hair shaking with mirth, the same long expressive hands gesticulating in front of her; but now the hair was white and the hands painfully distorted. They came to a clearing in the forest. There was a path leading off it down which only one could go. They stopped and turned to face each other, her mother smiled, stepping backwards onto the path and into the shade leaving Sandy alone in the sunlight. She began to cry and reach out to her mother who gently embraced her and then firmly with both hands held her daughter's head. Sandy could feel her fingers resting lightly on her temples and then the image of her mother started to fade as the pressure on her temples increased and she began to feel a warm glow radiating from her head and a feeling of well being.

She was woken from her dream by the sun streaming through a gap in the curtains onto her face. She had turned her head away from the glare and stared straight into the serene face of Mo in the photograph beside her bed – yes, today was going to be special.

From Baron's Court to Green Park she sang through the routine in her mind looking up and across the aisle at the end of the number into the eyes of a middle-aged couple who were staring at her curiously. She realised she must have been pulling faces and smiled at them both self-consciously.

Twenty minutes later, according to plan, Sandy entered the ladies toilet on the fourth floor of a large department store, a stone's throw away from the theatre where the audition was being held. She'd allowed herself half an hour to get ready. The ladies' toilet was tucked away behind the men's suits thus ensuring its lack of use. Why it wasn't a gents Sandy had never fathomed out. As usual the toilet was deserted; there were three lavatories in all: one a disabled, a couple of basins and a good-sized, well-lit mirror. It smelt of cigarette smoke; someone must have had a crafty fag; she had fortunately kicked the habit ten years before. Sandy took a comb out of her bag and set about plaiting her shoulder length, straight blond hair, weaving wire in between in order to make the plaits stand out like two handlebars from the side of her head. She sang through the number while she worked until she heard footsteps outside. Two women, one with a strident cockney accent and verbal diarrhoea entered, the other was born to be a listener.

'There's never anyone in here... Oh!' she said, throwing Sandy a hostile stare, 'Well not usually.' She sniffed the air suspiciously. 'Someone's been smoking in here – filthy habit.' She looked again at Sandy who shook her head in denial. 'I'm goin' in the disabled – can't stand them other two, not enough room to swing a cat – I'll limp if anyone complains.' She laughed at her own joke and tried to open the door to the disabled lavatory. 'Here – this door's stuck, give us a hand Phyllis.' There was a nervous cough from inside.

'There's someone in there Rhoda,' Phyllis hissed.

Sandy looked up surprised; she thought she'd been alone. Rhoda pushed the door open of the middle lavatory and said begrudgingly, 'I'll have to go in this one then. You go next door Phyllis.'

'I don't need to go, Rhoda, do I?'

Rhoda entered and closed the door still talking. 'You're lucky you are, Phyllis, you've got a strong constitution you have. I've got an irritable bladder. My husband calls it an "irritating bladder" – drives him mad. Do you know there isn't a toilet I don't know from here to King's Cross.'

Phyllis was clearly embarrassed at the non-stop flow of conversation accompanied by the equally non-stop flow from Rhoda's 'irritating bladder.' She cast a sideways glance at Sandy who was standing with her blond sticking out plaits completed painting freckles on her nose. Sandy grinned at her in the mirror. Phyllis dropped her eyes to the floor and looked relieved when Rhoda came out and walked over to the basin sprinkling water on her hands in a gesture of washing. The two women departed and Sandy looked at her watch. It was quarter to eleven, she had fifteen minutes till the audition, she must hurry. She let herself into the middle lavatory to change into her costume hanging her hat on the hook behind the door. She looked around in despair. She too had hoped to use the larger disabled loo with its wide window ledge to put her bag on. This was certainly going to be a tight squeeze.

Sandy was halfway out of the store, dressed as a cowgirl, when she remembered the cowboy hat on the back of the loo door. She stood wondering what to do. If she forgot the hat she would be exactly on time; each actress had been allocated twenty minutes for the audition. There were six of them in all, three an hour from ten till twelve.

'They've got to do some quick thinking babe.' Sam had informed her yesterday in his pseudo American accent. 'They want contracts signed by the end of the day.'

I must have the hat, she decided, turning and running back through the store, bounding up the escalators two steps at a time oblivious to the odd looks of the people she passed and unaware of the store detective who stood in front of her barring her way.

'What's your rush, miss?' Sandy reddened as he looked her up and down with blatant curiosity. He was a barrel-chested man on short stocky legs with the flattened face of an unsuccessful boxer. She knew she must look odd. She put her hand up to her head and realised that her plaits were standing out on end. She tugged them down.

'Oh please! Please don't stop me, I'm so late,' she said breathlessly. 'I've left my hat in the ladies' loo.'

'You sure it's not your horse!' He smirked enjoying his own humour and then stood aside to let her pass.

'Just mind how you go, you could knock someone over charging about like that,' he called after her already retreating figure.

She looked at her watch as she hurried past the men's suits; it was one minute to eleven.

'Oh God!' She hated being late, her heart was racing and she began to feel panicky. She reached the ladies just as a young woman came out pushing a sprawling child in a pushchair. He was immersed in chocolate and held out two chocolate-coated podgy fingers which he aimed at Sandy making a guttural explosion noise from the back of his throat. Sandy, unaware that she had just been shot, headed straight for the loo with the hat – it was occupied – she stood back, tears of frustration welling up. There was a flush and the door opened. A very large lady sidled out and then reached back in to pick up several enormous carrier bags with the name of the store printed on them. Sandy slipped in and reached up behind the door for the hat – it wasn't there. She flew out and looked accusingly at the large lady now washing her hands, the carrier bags at her feet.

'Excuse me.' The woman looked up. 'You didn't just happen to see a hat in there?' Sandy indicated the loo and peered menacingly at the lady's bags.

'I sorry, I no speak a-good English. What you say?' Sandy repeated the question very slowly using exaggerated gestures for the hat. The woman who was watching her intently suddenly broke into a smile. One of her front teeth was gold.

'Ah si!' she laughed, warmly doing the same gesture for the hat as Sandy. 'I give to bambino, he very happy. Bang! Bang!' She laughed again showing a glittering display of more gold teeth. Sandy looked at her glumly remembering with loathing the chocolate-coated child. The woman picked up her bags and still nodding and smiling left.

Sandy stood quietly for a moment; it was suddenly very cold, she shivered. She'd never felt less like a cocky American cowgirl in her life. She turned to leave.

It was then that she heard it; a long, low desperate moan. It came from behind the door of the disabled loo. Sandy hesitated for a second.

'None of your business girl – get the hell out of here!' she told herself starting to move off. It came again; a strange haunting sound followed by stifled gasps.

Sandy found herself rooted, unable to move, her temples began to throb gently. On impulse she turned and knocked quietly on the door.

'Is everything alright in there?' There was a gasp then silence. 'Please answer.' Still no reply. Sandy knew she should go, she could always call someone, that would be the most sensible thing to do, wouldn't it? Something stopped her as she felt an intense heat in her head despite the cold draught all around her. Without thinking she stepped into the adjacent loo, pulled down the toilet seat and climbed on to it. She grasped the top of the thin partition wall and on tiptoes stretched her head upwards, her eyes barely reaching over the top; what she saw took her breath away.

There, on the ledge with the window wide open, was a fragile white-haired figure. She was kneeling facing the street; her whole body trembling, one small elegant shoe lay pathetically on the ground, the other dangled loosely from her foot. She was edging forward onto the outside ledge, one hand with arthritic, nicotine stained fingers spread-eagled on the glass of the open window, the other clasping and unclasping a shredded tissue. Sandy's heartbeat became erratic, she sensed at any second the woman would find the courage to lurch herself forward and off the ledge. She felt a sickening sensation in her bowel as though she might lose control.

Involuntarily she heard herself saying, 'Mother' in a quiet but still audible voice above the roar of the indifferent traffic below. The woman's back arched and her head turned very slightly. Sandy said again, 'Mother.'

The woman brought her head further round in the direction of the voice, her eyes searching and puzzled. She looked like a hunted, cornered creature, solitary, broken. Her face was like delicate porcelain that had cracked with age. She suddenly closed her eyes and swayed towards the open void. With Herculean strength Sandy hauled herself upwards by hooking her elbows over the partition, her feet swinging off the toilet seat.

'Please Mother, don't! Don't let go, I need you. Please don't do it again,' she heard herself crying, tears streaming down her face. The woman brought one hand down on the ledge to steady herself, she opened her eyes and tried to focus them on what seemed like a sobbing child with pigtails hanging crab-like over the top of the partition wall.

'Be careful child, you might fall and hurt yourself.' Her voice was frail and quavery but Sandy knew she had connected.

'Please stay there,' Sandy said her face red with the effort of hanging on. 'Promise me you won't move till I get there?'

The woman nodded her head. Sandy dropped down and then lay on the toilet floor, praying that the gap under the partition would be wide enough to let her through.

A few seconds later Sandy had both her arms firmly round the woman's waist as she coaxed and eased her inwards and off the ledge.

'What's your name?' said Sandy when she'd finally brought her in, her face and make-up running with sweat from all the effort.

'Hannah,' she said. 'What's yours?'

'Sandra – but everyone calls me Sandy.'

'Sandy – I thought you were a child Sandy.'

'I am – inside.' Sandy grinned. 'I'm still waiting to grow up!'

'Me too,' Hannah replied, and then burst into tears. 'I'm sorry – so sorry,' she said between sobs. 'I was just so angry – I thought it was the answer.'

Sandy tore off some toilet paper and gave it to Hannah to blow her nose.

'It was the way he told me, so... so indifferent, so uncaring, as if, because I'm old, it didn't matter. Do you mind if I sit down a minute?' She lowered herself onto the closed toilet seat. Sandy waited silently for her to go on.

'He told me they might have to amputate my leg. He said it coldly, without any feeling.'

Sandy gulped. 'Who said that to you?'

'The consultant, I forget his name.'

'But why?' Sandy looked down at Hannah's bird-like legs.

'Bad circulation. I might get gangrene and unless I can...' She stopped speaking and her eyes welled up with tears again. 'I had to get out of there Sandy, so I stood up, looked him in the eye and said, "Over my dead body!" And then I stormed out. And I meant it until...' She looked up at Sandy shyly. 'Until I saw your little face peeping over the top. I realised I couldn't do that to my son...'

There was a sudden commotion outside as a door burst open. It was Rhoda's voice Sandy could hear above the others.

'In here officer. I saw it with my own eyes. We was leaving the store and I just happened to look up, didn't I Phyllis? She was kneeling on the edge...'

'How do you know it was in here?' the man's voice said.

''Cause I know all the toilets, inside and out, don't I Phyllis?'

Sandy stepped over to the door and half-opened it. She came face to face with the store detective. There was a look of recognition and disbelief on his face. Sandy's plaits were now completely upright.

'Oh it's *you*!' he said. 'What exactly is going on in here?'

'Nothing at all. Everything's perfectly fine.' Sandy smiled at him sweetly and tried to close the door but he put his foot in between and forced it open.

Sandy stared into a sea of faces and craning necks. She tried to screen Hannah from their view but the store detective pushed her aside leaving Hannah fully exposed on her cold, white throne. She was staring at the ground and Sandy could see her neck turning crimson above her collar. She knew she had to think quickly.

'Alright, now everyone's had a good look would you all mind going. My mother became unwell, she went to the window for some air – she happens to suffer from vertigo and she got stuck. O.K.?' Sandy folded her arms and stared up at the detective.

'On the outside ledge? Are you asking me to believe that?' His eyes narrowed.

'I'm not *asking* you to believe anything, I'm *telling* you that's what happened.' Sandy looked up at him fiercely. He returned her stare with equal hostility. The crowd outside had become silent. He turned towards Hannah whose face had now turned scarlet too.

'Madam, is what this young lady said true?'

'Yes,' she said quietly. 'I'm so sorry to have caused you all this fuss.'

He stood with his hands on his hips staring at them both. He turned towards Sandy. 'Hang on – you told me you'd left your hat up here – not your mother!'

'That's true,' she replied, 'I've still lost my hat – but I found my mother.'

Twenty minutes later the store detective bundled them into a cab. It was twelve-fifteen and, though Sandy knew she had missed the audition, she felt surprisingly calm.

They sat silently at first heading through the mid-day traffic towards St John's Wood. Hannah took her hand and patted it; she had a way of putting her head on one side before she spoke.

'Was that you I heard singing earlier on?'

'For my sins. I was practising for an audition, that's why I'm dressed like this.'

'You've got a lovely voice...' A worried look flickered across her face. 'I haven't made you late have I? I'm quite alright now you know, you don't have to stay with me.'

'No you haven't made me late.' Sandy thought quickly. 'It's not till two o'clock this afternoon and besides, I want to stay with you.'

Hannah patted her hand again. 'I feel as though I've known you all my life.'

They never stopped talking for the rest of the journey until they were standing outside Hannah's front door on the second floor of a smart block of mansion flats. Hannah put the key in the lock but, before she could turn it, the door flew open and a bearded giant of a man scooped her up in his arms.

'Where have you been, Mother? I came to the hospital to pick you up and they told me you'd walked out on your specialist. I've been worried sick!'

'I thought I'd told you not to come, you've got so much to do.'

'Since when have I listened to you,' he said affectionately. His voice was rich and deep.

Hannah reached for Sandy's hand. 'Aaron, I want you to meet Sandy. I don't know what I would have done without her today. She... she...' Her voice cracked with emotion. 'She's very special... I'm so happy she's come into my life.' Hannah's eyes had filled with tears.

Aaron turned and smiled warmly at Sandy. He was in his forties with an almost Biblical face and deep brown compassionate eyes.

'Then I'm really pleased to meet you,' he said.

'Me too,' said Sandy, wishing she wasn't wearing a cowgirl dress with her hair in plaits. He was immensely attractive.

An hour later they both waved her off in a mini cab shouting 'good luck' as she went. She was ensnared in her own white lie as she headed off for the audition. They had insisted on ordering and paying for the cab, Hannah so full of confidence on her behalf.

'When they hear you sing, my dear, you're bound to get the part.' Well at least she'd gained another fan.

She could have lingered there all day basking in the tenderness between a mother and her son. She longed to be a part of it.

After returning her costume and paying an exorbitant price

for the missing hat she was broke and decided to walk slowly back through the parks to Baron's Court. This would help to clear her head so full of mixed emotions and postpone the silence of her awaiting flat.

The answer phone was bleeping furiously as she let herself in. She sat wearily down on the arm of the sofa and switched the button on. There were four messages in all. The first two were from her agent: one asking her *where* she was as the management were *still* waiting for her even though she was *late*. The second call was less restrained and full of expletives and profanities. It ended with: 'Well all I can say, babe, is, you've really screwed up this time!' She nodded sadly. The third call made Sandy sit up: it was Aaron. He sounded shy and hesitant at first.

'Hi Sandy, Aaron here. Just wanted to know how things went. Mother says you've got the part – she's had one of her premonitions!' He laughed. 'I don't believe in premonitions but I'm forced to say she's nearly always right! Anyway I wanted to say 'thanks' for everything – you know – Mother told me what happened. I... er... well I wondered if I could take you out to dinner tomorrow or...sorry I'm a bit out of practice at this sort of thing. Anyway you're not there so I'll phone you later. Oh yes, one more thing, Mother rang the specialist to apologise and has promised him she's going to give up smoking. Bye for now.'

Sandy was so excited by this call that she wasn't concentrating on the last message until she realised it was her agent sounding quite contrite.

'Sandy, it's me again, Sam – are you there... obviously not!' He sighed. 'Listen to me, sweetheart, they *haven't* found their Goddamned Annie and they still want to see *you*! They've got some cockeyed idea that you might have been insulted being asked to audition! How do you like *that*! I told 'em you're the best Annie this side of the Atlantic and they seemed to agree – so where the hell are you for crying out loud! I'm dying of hunger here and I'm not moving till you phone!' He then added as an afterthought, slightly nervously: 'You're not dead, are you?'

Sandy lay in bed that night savouring the anticipation of the next day. Aaron was driving her to meet with the management of *Annie Get Your Gun*, then back to lunch with Hannah to tell her all about it, then out to dinner that night with Aaron and then… and then who knows!

Sandy turned over on her side and picked up the photograph of Mo and smiled. She replaced it on her bedside table and reached up to switch out the light but before she did she could have sworn that Mo smiled back and – who knows, perhaps she did!

CHANGING FACES

My last cigarette, Henrietta thought, inhaling deeply before blowing the smoke out of the window. One final act of defiance. She took the glowing stub to the bathroom and doused it under the tap before returning to the window, putting her hand out, and releasing it into the black Los Angeles sky. They were fifty stories up; it had a long way to go. She turned back into her pristine clinical room, the crisp white bed looked inviting but she had work to do and very little time to do it. She hurried over to the bedside cabinet, opened the drawer and took out a small tape recorder which she had purchased the day before. She sat on the bed and pushed the buttons. The man in the electrical store had explained how to work it as though to a child – so why wasn't it working? She fiddled with it some more and then threw it down on the bed with an anguished cry of despair. The door almost immediately opened and Florence, the night nurse, popped her head round and asked if everything was all right. She was from South Carolina and softly spoken.

Henrietta was close to tears as she picked up the tape recorder, waving it at the nurse.

'No, Florence, no. I'm shouting at this beastly little tape machine – it's brand new and it doesn't work. It's vitally important that I record something on it tonight otherwise...' Her voice trailed off as an internal panic set in. It had to work.

Florence came across the room, took the machine from her and examined it. 'What exactly have you been doing, Mrs Hastings?'

'I've been pressing the record button to record, and a red light should come on, but it doesn't – you try.'

Florence clicked some buttons and grinned. ;Mrs Hastings, honey, it don't work cause you ain't switched it on – see here – where it says "on and off"?'

'Hadn't I?! Oh how silly of me! I was assured it was foolproof – I suppose there are degrees of foolishness!'

They both laughed and chatted for a while, till Henrietta became aware of the time and looked anxiously at her watch.

Florence saw this and said, 'I must let you get some sleep, it's past midnight. You've got a big day ahead of you tomorrow.'

Henrietta nodded meekly and climbed into bed. 'You mean I need my *beauty* sleep?' She looked at Florence archly.

Florence laughed. 'That's good, I must remember that one!' She crossed to the door and laughed again '*Beauty* sleep! Goodnight now.'

Henrietta waved. 'Goodnight and thank you for being so kind to such a foolish old woman.'

The door clicked shut. Henrietta picked up the tape recorder and thought about what she was going to say. She conjured up the image of her daughter and in her mind placed her at the end of the bed. Zoe was an artist's dream with her parchment skin surrounded by a cluster of pre-Raphaelite Titian curls, her determined chin and piercing light blue eyes. Henrietta switched the machine on. She breathed in deeply and then began to speak slowly into the microphone:

'Zoe darling, it's your Mum. I've written you a long rambling

letter but I'm worried there are things in it that you might misconstrue, so I had this brainwave to make you a tape. I thought if you could actually hear me explain everything it might help you to understand and not be too angry with me.'

Henrietta laughed nervously and then coughed.

'Yes darling, I have just had a ciggie.' She could almost see Zoe's disapproving face. *'Funny isn't it – how roles reverse? Sometimes I feel as though I'm the child and you're my mother, but then they say old age is a slow slide back to infancy. I'm sitting up in bed in this very exclusive little hospital on the outskirts of Los Angeles – very different from Guildford Hospital; the nurses are not so rushed, you don't have to apologise when you want something. I can't pretend I'm not a little nervous – but I am certain I'm doing the right thing for everyone.'*

Henrietta paused for a moment. She needed to make this bit crystal clear.

'I don't want anyone feeling guilty – the only guilty one is **me**. *I've searched my conscience and I certainly don't. I suppose the idea took shape that day you took me to Guildford Hospital to get the results of my scan – must be at least six weeks ago.'*

Henrietta paused the tape, lay back against the pillows and tried to gather her thoughts together. Knowing you are going to die is a strangely liberating experience, after all no one is going to be let off the hook. Life's only certainty is death and she had the advantage of setting her house in order. She was not a religious person though certainly not an atheist, more 'a hopeful agnostic'. She reasoned with herself that if God exists and is as all loving and all caring as His believers proclaim then surely He would forgive her; but would her children?

She was seventy-seven years old, so already seven over the

allotted biblical time. She had lived something of a charmed, if somewhat selfish, life; perhaps the reason she had not found the need to search for the Almighty. She had been widowed twice and had enjoyed two truly amazing marriages to two equally brilliant but very different men. In fact if there was an afterlife this could be a cause for some concern: whose hand would she hold on all those heavenly walks? She had loved them both with equal passion. Perhaps He would allow a spiritual 'ménage a trois'. The thought made her smile.

She had an inoperable cancer – lung cancer – only herself to blame. The tumour had been discovered on her left lung and she was admitted for immediate surgery. However her heart had stopped as soon as the anaesthetic was administered. She was told that she was one of those rare people that can't take anaesthetic and it was a miracle that she was alive. She was at first reluctant to go through with the recommended treatment of radio and chemotherapy to delay, not cure, the cancer's progress but was finally persuaded to go ahead by her daughter Zoe. Henrietta had argued that she had had a good innings and her bags were packed but Zoe would have none of it; to her life was sacrosanct. Zoe was also a recent convert to alternative medicine and, like all converts, was a fanatic. She immediately put Henrietta on a stringent anti cancer diet: no toxins, no meat, not even fish. Caffeine, cigarettes and alcohol had to be things of the past. Henrietta went along with the new regime mainly to humour her daughter. It wasn't easy; she salivated every time she walked past the butchers. For a short while though she did begin to feel well again and even dared to hope that she was in full remission until the overwhelming tiredness returned but this time with the odd dizzy spell. She had gone to see Dr Mason, the oncologist, who ordered up another scan and that day, at Guilford Hospital, was to hear the results. She told Zoe it was for her three monthly check-up, and refused to let Zoe come in with her, aware the news might be bad but, if she were truthful, more worried that Zoe would propound her own theories on how to cure cancer. She had tactfully tried to tell her saying that Dr Mason simply would not have the time. Zoe had flared up.

'Then he should *make* the time, he might learn something and cut his work-load by half.' She had thrust out her chin, so like her father, pig-headed and arrogant.

Indeed the news was bad; the scan had shown up secondaries though the original tumour had shrunk to the size of a pea.

She smiled bravely at Dr Mason's strained face. 'Don't worry, Dr Mason, you warned me this would happen. How long have I got?'

He fiddled with his pen before answering. 'Cancer is a law unto itself, Mrs Hastings, there is no way I can answer that.'

'You mean,' she said teasingly, 'there is no way you are *going* to answer that. My first husband, he was a surgeon, always dreaded that question.'

'Because there are no definitive answers.'

'Let me put it another way,' she had persisted. 'I have some loose ends – rather important ones – to tie up before I pop off. Should I be getting on with those now or...' She let the question hang in the air.

Dr Mason rubbed his chin thoughtfully. 'I should get on with what you have to do. I recommend you have another three week course of radio therapy – that should hold things back a while.' He cleared his throat. 'You need to know where your secondaries are, Mrs Hastings.'

'Of course,' she said, assuming it would be her other lung.

He looked very grave. 'I'm afraid we found them in your brain.'

Henrietta began talking again into the tape recorder:

'When he told me the cancer had spread to my brain I just wanted to die there and then. I turned from this brave plucky woman and burst into tears. It threw him poor chap. I suppose my vision of dying had been 'Camille' like – me lying on the bed surrounded by my loved ones, my lungs slowly expiring while I comforted you all with my logical no nonsense approach to death. But suddenly that whole scenario changed: cancer in my brain, losing my mind, no longer being in charge of my life. He was desperate to call you in, Zoe, but I wouldn't let him. I made him promise not to tell you. I needed time to think. That was why I was so horrid to you in the car on the way home.'

She'd felt so guilty about that day deceiving her own daughter. She had told Zoe that the tumour had shrunk to the size of a pea, but omitted to tell her about the secondaries.

Zoe had whooped with delight when she heard the news. 'The size of a pea – I don't believe it.'

'But it hasn't gone,' Henrietta had said cautiously. 'I mean I do have to have more radiation.'

'Yes, but we're winning. Have you told him everything *we've* been doing?'

Henrietta was spared answering when a taxi shot out in front of them and Zoe slammed on the breaks.

Zoe suggested going to pick up Poppy, her daughter, from the antenatal clinic and they all go back to her house for a celebration tea.

Henrietta declined, using Toffee, her golden retriever, as an excuse. The last thing she felt like doing was celebrating. It was hard enough trying to look cheerful about her pea-sized tumour.

Zoe tried again. 'Toffee will be alright for another hour. Come on Mum!'

'Not today darling. I'd rather go straight home.'

There was a hurt silence before Zoe spoke. 'Do you know what Poppy said to me the other day? She said, "I think Granny's been avoiding me."'

Henrietta looked indignant. 'That is absolute nonsense and you know it.'

Zoe glanced sideways at her mother. 'Well you have been extremely po-faced about the baby.'

'If you call *po-faced* being concerned about my granddaughter, then yes, I have. I don't think either of you have thought it through properly.'

'Of course we have. If you had your way Poppy would have had an abortion.'

Henrietta sighed. 'Yes, I think it would have been more sensible. She's barely seventeen, extremely immature and she's flushing all that education down the...'

Zoe cut in angrily. 'Mum! You're forgetting something: we don't believe in abortion, it was never an issue.'

'You mean *you* don't,' Henrietta snapped back. 'I sometimes think Poppy is having this baby to please you.'

Zoe was incensed. 'Poppy's longing to have the baby. When it comes to human life you can't talk about being *sensible* – all life is sacred.'

Henrietta smiled sadly. 'Is it?' She felt so tired, 'Sorry darling, I don't feel that way.'

They drove the rest of the journey in silence. Zoe barely said 'good-bye' as Henrietta stepped out of the car and walked alone into her small stone cottage. Toffee bounded over to greet her.

'After you dropped me off I walked round the cottage in a complete daze. Toffee seemed to sense my mood and kept pushing her nose into my hand.

*Extraordinary how intuitive dogs are. We tried sitting in the garden but it made me feel isolated. I wish I had gone back to tea with you and Poppy. Instead I drowned my sorrows in alcohol. Its only effect was to make me more depressed and gave me a pounding headache. I thought I could feel the cancer inside my head scrambling my brain. I was consumed with guilt about my behaviour to you that afternoon- it was unforgivable. I've been so blessed to have you as my daughter. I don't know what I would have done without you since Michael died – you've made me feel **needed**. I can almost hear you saying "but you **are** Mum!"*

'And you've been a wonderful mum too Zoe, so much better than me. I never gave you and Leon that much time, too wrapped up in your father and then, after that, with Michael. I still dream about them both – quite sexy dreams. Oh yes, even at my age you can still dream! I fell asleep in the armchair and had the most horrendous nightmare. I was naked in the corner of the room on all fours snarling and growling like a mad dog at Toffee who was trembling in the other corner of the room. Foam was coming out of my mouth and I began to howl – the noise woke me up. It was Toffee howling to go out and I'd been dribbling in my sleep. I made a cup of tea and sat down at the table. It then came to me what I must do: I've always been in control of my life; I can be in control of my death too. I don't have to wait till the bitter end making you all suffer.

'Suddenly I felt very calm. I would know when the time was

*right. What worried me was **how** I was going to do it. I went upstairs to bed and found myself looking at all the photos of you and Leon as children.*

'Do you remember that one of Leon standing in his new school uniform aged eight? We took it the day he went off to boarding school. He was trying desperately hard to smile but behind those ghastly specs he used to wear was a look of sheer terror. We should never have sent him, he had a rotten time. I started to go over the whole Leon saga in my mind. I knew I must try and put things right between us before I carried out my plan. That's why I came round to see you the next day. I was totally unprepared for your reaction.'

Henrietta stopped the tape and poured herself a glass of water.

She had gone round on the bus first thing in the morning. Zoe would be at home studying for her PhD in psychology and Gus would have left for work. Zoe was surprised to see her and a little frosty, but when Henrietta said she was hoping she could take Poppy out for lunch her whole demeanour changed – all was forgiven.

'How lovely, Mum, I'll go and wake her up. She's getting as much sleep in as she can before the baby comes.'

'Please don't wake her,' Henrietta said. 'I wanted to have a chat with you first – on our own.'

Zoe had linked arms with her and led her into the large kitchen where the table was littered with textbooks, a laptop, mounds of screwed up paper and pads filled with notes in Zoe's illegible, chaotic handwriting.

Zoe made them both a cup of mint tea, ignoring Henrietta's plea for a real builders' brew. She then sat down at the table, sweeping her work to one side, and said in that direct way she had, 'So Mum, talk. You look very tired.'

Henrietta nodded. 'I am. I didn't sleep a wink last night, too much on my mind.' She hesitated a moment, no point beating about the bush. 'I've come to a big decision which you're not going to like.'

Zoe stretched across the table and clasped her mother's hand. 'Please don't say you are going to give up Mum – please – not now.'

Henrietta had looked across at the distraught, beautiful face of her daughter, devoid of any make-up. She was forty-seven, such an independent and feisty woman and yet still so needy of her mother. Zoe would soon be a grandmother, Henrietta thought. Perhaps with a new young life in her life she'll start to let go of mine.

'No, I'm not giving up, not yet. I want to go to Los Angeles to see Leon.'

Zoe pulled her hand away and stared in disbelief at her mother. 'Leon! Tell me you're joking.'

'No, I'm quite serious. I must try and make my peace with him.'

'Whatever for?'

'He *is* my son Zoe.'

'He forfeited those rights a long time ago.'

'No darling, your children are for life, whatever they do.'

'That's bullshit Mum!' Zoe stood up, angrily gathered up the cups, stomped over to the kitchen sink and turned the tap on. 'He's hung up on you every time you've tried to ring him, he's ignored your letters... he never even got in touch with you after Michael died.'

Henrietta stared at Zoe's rigid back. 'No, but in fairness he didn't know, did he?'

'Of course he knew, because I wrote and told him.' Zoe was still rinsing out the cups furiously.

Henrietta felt like she had been stabbed. 'Really? Did you really? I wonder why he didn't call.'

Zoe spun round almost ranting, 'Because, Mum, he's a heartless pig – an unfeeling, uncaring, selfish, thoroughly unpleasant human – or should I say non-human being...'

'Goodness!' Henrietta said. 'Yesterday you were talking about all life being *sacred.*'

'I didn't say I wanted to kill him.' she retorted. 'But I never want to see him again.' She returned to the table and sat down. 'Anyway, suppose he doesn't want to see *you,* have you thought about that?'

Indeed she had, and she certainly wasn't going to force herself upon him, nor was she going to tell him she was dying. He must only see her because he wanted to. It was 20 years since he'd gone off unannounced to the States. The only contact since had been the annual printed Christmas card from which she gleaned he had remarried and had two children, her grandchildren, whom she had never met. Leon would be 50 next month.

'Maybe age has softened him,' she said hopefully. 'And I'd like to meet my grandchildren too.'

'They won't even know who you are.'

'Probably not,' Henrietta agreed, 'but it's not their fault is it? I was thinking about it all again last night. I should have been more aware of his feelings.'

'Sentimental rubbish, Mum. I could have reacted the same way but I didn't!'

Of course she didn't. At that time Zoe had been too wrapped up in her own love life, which was always eventful with a stream of highly unsuitable, mostly married, older men. Looking for her father perhaps.

'You know what, Mum, Leon should have been happy for you finding love again after Daddy died, instead of behaving like an adolescent kid. He was thirty for Christ's sake! What did he want you to do: sit around in mourning for the rest of your life?'

'He was going through a difficult time. He was very mixed up.'

'Oh *please*,' Zoe groaned. 'You've always made excuses for him, Mum. Even when he was little you let him get away with murder.'

Yes, maybe she had, through guilt. She had never quite bonded with her son like she had with Zoe, so perhaps she had over-indulged him to compensate for what she didn't always feel inside.

'I think you're forgetting, Zoe, what a sickly and delicate child he was.'

Henrietta and Arthur were sleep deprived for the first three years of Leon's life. So much so that when she discovered she was pregnant with Zoe – not a planned pregnancy – she and Arthur had spent a whole day after one particularly disturbing night discussing whether to go through with it or not. She had never dared tell Zoe that her little life once hung in the balance. Thank God they decided not to terminate. Zoe was like a breath of fresh air, the perfect baby: slept, gurgled and was utterly gorgeous. Of course Leon had to be indulged.

Henrietta looked across the table at her daughter. 'Leon changed you know. He wasn't always cold.'

'Oh yes he was!' Zoe said. 'I remember that time when we were in Majorca. Leon was about 10. He stalked this tiny lizard and decapitated it with a hard boiled sweet.'

Henrietta laughed. 'Oh for heaven's sake! Little boys are often cruel – it's in their make-up.'

'No, Leon was a wimp, couldn't say boo to a goose – but you should have seen the look of triumph on his face when he showed me that helpless little lizard.'

Henrietta remembered the incident; they were sitting by the pool and Zoe had brought over the decapitated lizard and put it on Arthur's lap. She was in tears. 'Please Daddy, can you sew his head back on? Leon says you can.' Leon was standing behind Zoe looking rather sheepish.

'No princess,' his pet name for Zoe, 'I'm afraid Daddy can't mend him.'

Leon butted in shouting, 'Yes you can, Dad, you can mend anything.' He pointed at Michael spread out on a sunlounger. 'Uncle Michael says you're the best surgeon in the world.'

Zoe had begun to cry inconsolably and was not to be placated until they had carried out a formal burial beneath the pine trees and Leon had been suitably reprimanded.

'We used to have lovely holidays all together with Michael and Pat, didn't we?' Henrietta said, hoping to discourage Zoe from any further character assassination of her brother.

This only added fuel to the fire. 'Exactly!' she said. 'So why did he turn against Michael? He used to adore him when he was a kid.'

'Yes darling. It was a wonderful friendship, more like an extended family, but when my relationship with Michael changed it must have seemed to Leon like incest. We should have waited a little longer, given him time to adjust to the idea.'

'Why?' Zoe said. 'It was perfect – Michael had lost Pat, you'd lost Dad. You had a chance of happiness again – you were right to grab at it.'

Yes, that was exactly how she had felt at the time, not a minute to lose. As it turned out they only had 10 precious years together before Michael had a fatal stroke and died, so surely she was right to push ahead wasn't she, despite sacrificing the relationship with her only son? But now, hopefully, there was still time to put that right.

The sad thing was that, during Arthur's illness, Leon and Henrietta had become closer than they had ever been before. Leon had come round frequently to sit with his father. Michael was often there too, helping Arthur complete his memoir on being one of the pioneers of liver transplant surgery. She used to hear the three of them laughing together upstairs. Leon would often stay on for supper. He had even confided in her about the breakdown of his marriage.

'You know, Zoe, Leon was at a very low ebb during that time – Daddy's illness, his divorce being made final. She took him to the cleaners.'

'Yes – well - we all warned him about her,' Zoe said unsympathetically.

'You're a fine one to talk, madam, the amount of men we warned you about! Since time immemorial, when have children ever listened to their parents' advice on the opposite sex?'

Zoe acknowledged the snub with a rueful grin.

'You were just lucky,' Henrietta continued, 'that Gus came into your life and took you and Poppy on.'

'You mean *he* was lucky,' Zoe said firmly, and meant it.

That was the difference between her two siblings: one so confident, the other riddled with complexes. She and Arthur had to accept some blame.

Henrietta sat back in her chair and folded her arms. 'The

trouble with Leon,' she said, 'is he never had any self-confidence. Your Dad didn't help matters constantly, ribbing him for becoming an oral surgeon and not following in his footsteps.'

'Leon was probably scared he wouldn't be as good as Dad,' Zoe said.

This was true. Leon had told her he became tongue tied in his father's presence. Arthur was so erudite and witty it made him feel like a total nerd.

'Leon was in awe of Arthur. It's sad to be frightened of your own father.'

'I never was.' Zoe put her hand up to her mouth. 'Sorry that sounded really smug.'

Henrietta laughed affectionately. Zoe had been the apple of her father's eye, his little princess. She could twist him round her little finger but then so could she until Arthur's illness. When he was first diagnosed with bowel cancer and told he would have to undergo major surgery he had been quite calm: organised his own operation, the surgeon he wanted and insisted that Michael would be his anaesthetist. That terrible phone call from the hospital after the operation was etched on her memory; the cancer had spread through to his liver and beyond. Arthur returned home to die. Henrietta was beside herself with grief ready to nurse and love him through the whole dreadful ordeal but he wouldn't allow it, insisted on having a nurse. He wouldn't let her change the dressings or see his disfigured body even though she had been a nurse when they had first met. He sometimes looked at her so strangely when she came into the room; perhaps he resented that she was going on and he wasn't. She, who had been the love of his life, was suddenly pushed out of his limelight and it was crucifying.

'What are you thinking about, Mum?' Zoe said. 'You look

so sad.'

'I was remembering those last few awful months. Daddy was very cruel to me you know.'

'You've never told me that,' Zoe said.

'It was all part of the illness I suppose, it made him bitter. It was terrible for him to stop working so abruptly…it was like…' She looked up at the ceiling trying to find the right analogy.

'God losing his power overnight.' Zoe added helpfully.

Henrietta smiled. 'Exactly! Well he was known as *King Arthur* behind his back. Michael said your father was the most skilful surgeon he had ever worked with. "A genius" he said.'

'They were quite a team, weren't they – Dad and Michael?'

Henrietta nodded. 'And yet so different. Michael was more approachable, more simpatico, probably easier for anaesthetists – they don't have to carve people up do they?'

'Who do you think about more? Michael or Daddy?' Zoe had suddenly asked.

It was a hard question to answer. These days she lived constantly in the past, less daunting than her future. Michael would have been a good person to grow old with. Arthur was more exciting, a tireless lover, unpredictable and at times challenging, a Macho Male with a capital M. Whereas Michael was at peace with himself and the world: a sensual and aesthetic man, always aware of the feelings of his fellow human beings.

'It depends on my mood,' she answered finally.

Zoe reached across the table and took Henrietta's hand. 'You're not really going to go to Los Angeles are you Mum?'

'I must see Leon, Zoe …there are things I have to put right between us. There's something I should have told you about, something you ought to know.'

Zoe remained silent, watching her mother twisting the two

wedding rings she always wore.

'Leon thought that Michael and I were having an affair while Daddy was still alive.'

Zoe was immediately on guard. 'I see. But you weren't, were you?' She suddenly raised her hand. 'Actually – don't tell me! I'd rather not know.'

Henrietta chewed on her lip before she spoke. 'It was a cerebral affair. There were moments, intimate moments, a touch, a look – and an overwhelming desire – but no, we didn't make love till after Daddy died.'

Michael had been the strong-minded one, not her. Michael was far too honourable and loyal to betray his friend.

Zoe looked relieved. 'Well, there you are then, unfortunately we can't censor our subconscious desires, only suppress them which you rightly did.' She tapped a dense psychology book lying on the table. 'It's all in there. Lets have another cuppa, shall we?' She walked over to the kettle and switched it on.

Henrietta longed for a cigarette. 'There's something else I have to tell you Zoe.'

'Oh dear! More suppressed desires?' Zoe turned round and leaned back against the sink. 'Go on then, spit it out.'

'When Arthur turned against me and became so cold I unburdened myself on Michael. I'm afraid I started to fall in love with him then.'

She had wanted him so much sometimes it physically hurt.

'And Michael, did he feel the same?'

'Oh yes, it was mutual. He even suggested he stayed away. I begged him not to – he did your father so much good – and me. The whole atmosphere in the house changed when he was there.'

'Did Leon sense what was happening to you both?'

'Absolutely not. He and Michael were getting on like a house on fire. It was after Daddy died that it all went wrong.'

'What happened?' Zoe asked.

Henrietta put her head in both hands staring down at the table and spoke in a low monotone. 'It was about two weeks after, not more. Michael had come for supper and stayed over. I had asked him to. It was the first time. We'd had quite a bit to drink and I was concerned about him driving. Leon turned up next morning unexpectedly at the house. He had his own key and we didn't hear him coming in. I wasn't downstairs so he came upstairs to find me. The bedroom door was open and... he saw us...'

Zoe gasped in horror. 'You weren't...'

Henrietta nodded gravely.

She was standing by the window sipping water, looking out over the sprawling mass that was Los Angeles below her. She could feel herself becoming hot at the thought of it all over again: *caught in the act, in flagrante delicto.* That's how Leon had seen her. They had all frozen for a split second before Leon had charged out of the room and down the stairs. Michael had quickly dressed and discreetly disappeared allowing her to have a talk with Leon. She had found him in the kitchen, white as a sheet, his large nose was red, a sure sign that he was stressed and his eyes were pink and glistening behind the heavily lensed spectacles he wore. He was sitting on a stool that was too small for his lanky body. Henrietta had wanted to take him in her arms and comfort him but when she took a step towards him he warned her off with his hand and said, 'Don't say anything – it never happened!' He had left the house, almost shattering the front door.

She had written him a letter of apology asking for his understanding, and to come and see her and talk things through.

His reply was final. He never wanted to see her again. She was a two-timing bitch, even worse than his wife. Michael went round to see him and was given the same treatment. Leon even accused them both of hastening Arthur's death for their own carnal depravity.

Michael, who was an understanding man, thought Leon would come round eventually, but he never did, and her marriage to Michael, a year after Arthur's death, was tinged with sadness. She would so have loved him and Michael to be friends again.

Henrietta looked at her watch, hurried back to the tape-recorder and picked it up sitting down on the edge of the bed:

'You were amazing that morning Zoe, so non judgemental. I felt cleansed. I've always envied Catholics being able to purge their souls at the confessional. I should have talked to you about it a long time ago. I suppose it was guilt that stopped me, or was it shame? I was ashamed of my behaviour. So it was easier to blot the whole thing out. You were so sweet wanting me to make the call to Leon from your house so that you could hold my hand, bless you. But I needed more than a hand, darling – I have to confess to several cigarettes and two stiff drinks before I had the courage to do it. Forgive me. I was so sure I would be snubbed again. I'd rehearsed every scenario in my mind but the one that happened.'

A woman with an American accent answered the phone.

'Hi there! Sea Changes. Can I help you?' The timbre of her voice was friendly and mellifluous, but the drink had done nothing to steady Henrietta's nerves; its only effect was to make her speech a little slurred. She tried to annunciate carefully.

'Oh! Hello.' How was she to announce herself? 'This is –

er – I'm – er...who am I speaking to?' she finally stammered.

'It's Melanie Lipscomb. Who wants to know?' the woman replied. 'Hey, are you selling something? You don't sound like a sales person?'

'Goodness no!' Henrietta laughed. 'I'm your mother's son.' No, that didn't sound quite right, she had better start again. 'I'm my son's mother.'

A short silence was followed by a deafening squawk. 'What?!!'

'I'm Leon's mother,' Henrietta tried again.

'Oh my gosh!' the voice was now breathless with excitement. 'His *English* mother from *England* ?'

'Well as far as I know I'm the only one he's got.'

Melanie was in a state of high excitement as she called for Leon to come to the phone urgently. Henrietta had held her breath while she waited, praying that he would speak to her.

His voice was cool and unemotional when he picked up the phone and said, 'Hello Mother.'

'Please don't cut me off,' she said, 'not this time.'

'I don't intend to,' Leon said. His voice had acquired a pseudo American accent. 'How are you Mother?'

'Fine, fine – getting older you know. I'm phoning because – well, because I thought it was high time to – er – to...'

'Patch up our relationship?' Leon said helpfully.

'Oh yes. Can we put the past behind us? Try and start again?'

'It won't be easy, but I think we could at least try. Can you come here to L.A.?'

The rest of the conversation had been brief. She had told him she could not come immediately due to certain prior commitments. She did not tell him about the radiotherapy she was about to undergo. He had insisted they would book it all up from their end and she must be their guest. He had then excused himself as he had a patient waiting for him.

'I was a bundle of nerves the morning you all took me to the airport. After kissing you "goodbye" I didn't dare look back. I think I would have lost my courage and not gone through with it. I was so touched that Poppy came too. The flight was marvellous. Leon had booked me into first class – what a difference! I actually managed to sleep. I spent my waking hours trying to visualise Leon as a middle-aged man. I wondered if I should kiss him.' Henrietta chuckled. *'Remember how funny he was about kisses? Always turning his head away at the last minute and left one kissing air! We landed in Los Angeles in a thick fog. The plane just suddenly seemed to hit the ground so I was bit wobbly on the old pins and my heart was going like a dingbat. Anyway I had some of that rescue remedy you gave me and had managed to calm down a little by the time I came through the barriers where Leon had told me he would be waiting. I looked around but didn't see him. A man appeared to be waving at a very obese woman who was standing next to me. She ignored him so I looked round to see who he was waving at. Then I heard him calling out, "Mother – Mother here! I'm over here!" So I turned back and this stranger bounded over to me and put both his hands on my shoulders and said, "Mother! How are you?"'*

It was a surreal moment, standing there not knowing her own son. She had said tentatively, 'Leon? Is that you?'

He had burst out laughing. 'Who else would be calling you mother, Mother? Of course it's me. Welcome to L.A.'

Henrietta smiled wanly. 'Oh my dear! I'm so sorry. I just

didn't recognise you – not a very good start is it?'

He told her she was forgiven, that twenty years was a long time. He then gathered up her luggage and asked her about the flight while leading her to the airport's exit.

Henrietta put her hand on his shoulder to attract his attention. 'Please stop a moment. Let me look at you properly.'

She scrutinised his face. 'You look completely different, and so young!'

He gave her a dazzling smile, the whiteness of his teeth enhanced by his tanned, unlined face. 'Why thank you, I certainly feel it.'

He went to walk on but Henrietta had remained stationery. She looked bewildered. 'But I don't understand – your face – it's changed, it doesn't look…well, it doesn't look like *you*. Am I going mad?'

Leon was clearly enjoying the moment before he spoke. 'No Mother, you're not going mad. I changed it a long time ago. Come to think of it, there's not an original feature left.'

'I actually fainted. He looks a bit like Larry Hagman when he played JR in Dallas – remember Zoe – you loved that series? Even his eyes have changed colour, they're a vivid blue now. I think he should have warned me, don't you? I told him so but he said he'd wanted to surprise me, he thought I'd be pleased – but why should I be pleased that my son has changed his face? It was a dreadful shock. He's very good looking now, but he's not my Leon. He used to have such an interesting face, full of character. I used to tell him that when he was growing up.

It was an awkward journey in the car. There was so much to say and yet we seemed to talk mostly about the weather – how repressed we English are. Melanie was waiting for us on the

*terrace outside the house though house is quite the wrong way
to describe it – more like a shimmering, low domed palace.
Everything's white – blindingly so – white pillars, white marble
floors, white carpets, white leather furniture and so much glass;
walls of glass rather than windows. And the whole place is built
round the swimming pool. Leon had to dash back to his hospital
to check on a patient and so left me and Melanie to become
acquainted. She was charming, really pretty and put me in mind
of somebody, but I couldn't for the life of me think who it was.'*

Henrietta was still sitting on the side of her bed; her one foot
had gone to sleep. She wiggled it up and down and then rotated
it back to life before standing up and walking round her little
room to get her circulation flowing. She returned to the bed and
sat down again listening to that brief interlude of stillness that
befalls a hospital in the small hours of the morning. That first
day in L.A. was still vivid in her mind.

Henrietta was treated to a guided tour of their palatial and
thankfully air-conditioned home. They were soon joined by
Roxanne, Leon and Melanie's 12-year-old daughter, who burst
out of a bathroom like a torpedo furious with her mother for not
calling her. She was an attractive child whose looks were only
slightly marred by silver braced teeth. She sizzled with high-
octane energy, talking rapidly without seeming to draw breath.

'I'm Roxy, I'm your granddaughter – it's so fantastic, you're
my grandmother – I can't believe it – it's like – wow – it's so
weird – it's like one minute you were dead and now suddenly
you're alive and I'm like so excited I couldn't sleep last night.
What do we call you – we call our other grandma 'Gaga', she's
82 – how old are you?'

'Roxy! You don't ask people that!' Melanie had cried.

Henrietta eased the situation by saying at 77 she was past caring people knowing how old she was.

'Now does this old grandma get a hug?' She smiled holding out her arms to Roxanne who stepped forward, allowing Henrietta to embrace her.

'How do you get to be so thin?' Roxanne said looking up at her. 'I'd love to be like you.'

'No you wouldn't dear. I'm skin and bones. You look just right to me.'

Henrietta patted her reassuringly.

'But I feel really gross and...' Melanie cut her short and threw open a door, announcing that this was to be Henrietta's room.

It was spacious, bright and welcoming. Henrietta was thrilled.

'What a magnificent room, Melanie. Look at the size of the bed. I shall get lost in it!'

'It's a waterbed, we've all got 'em,' Melanie said. 'You'll sleep like a baby; it's like going back to the womb – isn't it Roxy?'

'I don't remember,' Roxanne said twiddling her hair.

Henrietta was distracted by a double-framed photograph on the dressing table. She went over, picked it up and took a closer look.

'What a lovely photograph of you, Melanie.' She put the frame down and then picked it up again and said, triumphantly, 'Ah! I know now who it is you remind me of. Natalie Wood! Is that your sister on the other side of the frame?'

Melanie looked coy. 'No. Actually they're both me – before and after – so to speak.'

Henrietta looked mystified. What was she talking about?

'Before and after what dear?'

'Mom's plastic surgery,' Roxanne chipped in. 'Mom changed

her face to please Daddy. It really freaked my brother out. He wouldn't, like, go near Mom for 6 months. Luke's a screwball anyway.'

'Roxy that's enough! I changed my face because I wanted to.'

'But Daddy shows your photos to all his new patients because, it's like – he does it to his wife – it's like – it's got to be ok – yeah?'

Henrietta was flummoxed. 'I'm sorry, I'm lost. Why should Leon show your photos to patients he's going to perform oral surgery on?'

Suddenly the penny dropped and Melanie shrieked, 'Oh for heavens sake! Hasn't Leon told you yet?' She proceeded to tell Henrietta that her son was now a renowned plastic surgeon.

'I was really beginning to wonder if I was in a dream or if the cancer in my brain had finally taken hold and I was losing the plot. Thankfully they left me in my room so I could have a much-needed rest. The waterbed made me feel queasy so I took my pillows and stretched out full-length on the carpet. Melanie told me that Leon decided to retrain in plastic surgery after he'd had his own face done – it so transformed his life he wanted to do the same for other people. He's now considered a visionary in the field of plastic surgery, people come to him from all over the world; he remoulds faces using techniques no one has used before. I was just drifting off to sleep when I remembered something really rather alarming: when Leon was about fifteen he had a large poster of Natalie Wood stuck on the back of his bedroom door. I can't help wondering if Melanie changed her face to fulfil his fantasy. I was woken by a pair of eyes burning into me like two hot coals and an unpleasant chewing sound.'

Henrietta was staring up into the eyes of a small tubby boy of nine.

'Goodness me! You gave me a fright.'

He glared at her, his mouth relentlessly rotating, and said, 'Are you really my grandmother?' She felt exposed lying there in her petticoat, and tried to haul herself up to a more dignified position and sound agreeable at the same time.

'Indeed I am, if you are Luke.'

She had a cramp in her calf and grimaced with pain. Luke folded his podgy arms and screwed up his eyes. 'Why are you so old and ugly?'

'Because,' Henrietta said finally, standing up and reaching for her dressing gown lying on the bed and slipping it on, 'that's the way God made me.' She tied the belt firmly and stared back at him.

'We don't believe in God.' His look was challenging.

'Well we none of us know for sure, do we?' she said, trying to sound reasonable.

'Dad does. Why were you lying on the floor?'

'Because, Luke, I wanted to. So?' she said brightly changing the subject. 'What have you been doing today?'

'With my shrink. You're weird. I'm going for a swim.' He turned and rushed out of the room without so much as a backwards glance.

Henrietta had walked over to the full sized mirror built into the wardrobe and observed her face dispassionately. Did she really look 'so old and ugly?' She had always felt good about herself. Both Arthur and Michael made her feel beautiful and told her so and even Zoe, on the morning of her departure, had said that she looked 'stunning'. Of course she knew that it meant she looked good for her age. Her hair was cut boyishly short and had grown back white after the chemotherapy; the style emphasised her square-cut jaw line but also her scrawny neck. Her hand fluttered up to hide it. Her features were bold: wide set green eyes, a prominent nose and a generous mouth. The face no longer matched her painfully thin body. She turned away in despair wondering what to wear for dinner.

'It took me ages to decide what to wear that first night; everything I put on seemed to look awful, even some of my favourite outfits. I finally opted for my good old kaftan. I was very nervous and swigged down some more of the rescue remedy before joining them. They were already seated at this huge, glass oval table when I came in. Leon immediately got up and led me round to my place. Melanie had really gone to town and prepared a magnificent feast. I was seated opposite Betty, Melanie's mother. She's a pretty little woman – all her features turn upwards as though she's been strung from the top of her head on a giant meat-hook. She kept smiling at me and I kept smiling back, until I realised the smile was a permanent fixture. She recently had a stroke so doesn't talk and needs help with her food. Roxanne was supposed to be doing that, but I couldn't help noticing that she kept sneaking food off her own plate and popping it into her grandmother's mouth. It confirmed my earlier suspicion that she might be anorexic. It was a jolly party, even Leon appeared more relaxed – you wouldn't know him Zoe, he's so confident and sure of himself. They wanted to hear all about you and our life in England, if we're weathering the recession – he obviously is! It wasn't till the subject of age came up that it all became a little bit heated.

Leon had offered me some more red wine but I declined saying I didn't think I should. He said 'nonsense,' that red wine was good for you and keeps you young. I joked back that nothing could do that anymore. He then pointed across at Betty and said, 'You wouldn't know she was eighty-two, would you?' I had to agree, it would have been churlish not to. Melanie cleared the table ordering Luke to help, and a huge row erupted between him and Roxanne when he pointed out that Gaga hadn't eaten her meal. She smiled unperturbed through it all as Luke stomped out to the kitchen with her full plate of food.'

Henrietta poured herself some more water and took a sip; her mouth had gone quite dry. She checked her watch. It was 3.30 in the morning, time was marching on. She recalled her conversation with Leon.

Leon had leant over to her and said, 'In California no one has to be old anymore.'

'What's wrong with being *old*, Leon?' Henrietta had asked quite innocently.

His blue eyes opened wide in amazement. 'You're not serious are you Mother? You do know that we are living on the very brink of eternal life?'

'I know I am, dear, but not you surely, you're not fifty yet!'

'I'm talking about eternal life in this life – not some mythical eternity! What was once science fiction will soon be a reality.'

'What a dreadful thought', Henrietta said.

Roxanne looked perplexed. 'Why don't you want to live for ever – it's like – it's so sad – why should anyone want to *die* anyway?'

Henrietta answered her gently. 'Because when you reach my age, Roxy, you're tired – tired of life, hard for you to imagine. I can't think of anything worse than living on and on, looking and feeling as I do.'

'Agreed,' Leon said, 'but that's where I come in – using plastic surgery to keep my patients looking good until such time, and my guess is within the next twenty years or so, when we'll be able to halt the aging process – no one need die of old age anymore.'

'Won't our planet become a little overcrowded?' Henrietta suggested 'Or is the luxury of longevity to be limited to the chosen few?'

Leon nodded. 'In the beginning, yes.'

Henrietta felt provocative and suggested that perhaps in the beginning *God* had created the heaven and the earth.

Leon told her she was too intelligent to believe in God.

'Maybe not God necessarily,' Henrietta conceded, 'but a force stronger than ourselves, yes.'

Leon thumped his chest. 'Man is the only force – our future lies with Man, not God.'

'Then God help us!' Henrietta said quietly. 'I'm glad I won't be around. We should be trying to develop as human beings, not worrying about the way we look.'

'We can do both, but we live in a *visual* world, we're judged on how we look and we no longer – thanks be to *Man* – have to allow nature to decide our fate.'

Roxanne, who had been listening intently, piped up excitedly. 'Dad's going to give me the look of Julia Roberts when I graduate.'

Melanie came back into the dining room carrying dessert plates and placed them on the table. She turned to Roxanne. 'I heard that young lady – not unless you get good grades, remember?'

Henrietta was appalled. 'You're not really going to mess around with Roxy's face?'

Leon rose angrily from the table, his eyes had a messianic look, 'I do not *mess* around, Mother. I can assure you I am extremely skilled at what I do, probably as skilled as Father was in his field of work, maybe even more so...'

Of course. She should have realised; not only did Leon want to play God, but to emulate his father as well!

'And *yes,*' Leon continued zealously, 'I will give Roxy the image that she wants. If it makes her feel good about herself then she can conquer the world. What father would deny his daughter that?'

At that moment Luke returned carrying the dessert. Melanie announced that as this was a special day she was serving up the traditional pecan pie. Henrietta's stomach heaved at the thought of it.

Leon sat back down and smiled at Melanie. 'My wife makes the best pecan pie in California. Put it down here son.' Luke placed the dish on the table in front of his father. Leon reached out and pulled Luke next to him. 'Tell your grandmother what you would like to be.'

Luke grinned. 'I'd like to be a tiger then everyone will be frightened of me.' Luke did a surprisingly good imitation of a tiger growling. He looked at Roxanne. 'I'd kill you first Roxanne!' He growled again. Everyone fell about laughing except Henrietta, who was still reeling from the previous discourse.

Leon started to serve the pecan pie. 'Don't look so worried, Mother, I'm not that skilled!'

'I found it hard to digest the pecan pie. Couldn't wait to excuse myself and retire to my swaying bed where I tossed and turned all night – I was a premature baby; perhaps I hadn't liked

*the womb! The next day Leon was taking me out – just the two
of us – to a beautiful restaurant high up looking out over the
ocean. But first we walked along the beach; we both knew the
time had come for us to talk. I've always loved the sea, it's so
timeless, so neutral, it belongs to everyone and yet to no one.'*

Henrietta stood up and walked over to the window. How she
would have loved to be looking at the sea right now just one
more time.

They had walked in silence watching the waves breaking and
foaming up on to the sand. Henrietta had spoken first.

'You put an ocean between us, didn't you Leon? I never
understood how you were able to cut yourself off so completely.'

'I severed the umbilical cord. It was easier that way.'

'Easier than talking? Easier than trying to understand?'

'While Michael was still around – never!' He did not look at
her but just kept walking.

Michael was such a lovely man, it was so unjust, how could
anybody hate him? Leon had once loved him too. She tried to
say so.

'He betrayed my father,' Leon said coldly and without
emotion.

'But he didn't,' Henrietta cried. 'It wasn't like that, though
it may have seemed like that to you.'

'He practically lived in our house the year before Father
died – I can't believe I didn't see what was going on.' He was
controlling his anger.

Henrietta remained calm. 'Nothing was going on, Leon.
Michael was the only person who could lift your father's spirits,
they understood each other. It was him who motivated Dad to
write his book.'

Leon let out a derogatory snort. 'The miracle of the human mind: rearranges the past to ease its conscience.'

No, she had not rearranged the past. She was guilty of desire, that's all. Zoe had understood.

'My conscience is clear, Leon. It's you who has interpreted the past wrongly.'

Leon stopped and turned to face her angrily. 'Bullshit, Mother! I saw you *at it* – in the same bed Father died in, remember?'

'It was dreadful for you, for all of us,' she said.

'Michael was his best friend. He stood at the end of that *same* bed ten days before and watched him die.'

'Why didn't you shout at me that morning – we could have had it out, I could have tried to make you understand.'

'It was worse than finding my wife in bed with another man. It shattered everything that I believed in.'

Henrietta looked at her son and felt a sudden rush of compassion for him. 'Oh my dear – I'm so sorry that it happened the way it did.' She paused, trying to choose her words carefully. 'But what I want you to try and understand is that year of your father's illness was very difficult for me.'

'Difficult for you, impossible for Father.'

She tried to explain that Arthur had turned away from her both physically and mentally. 'It was as though he wanted me to hate him as much as he hated himself.'

'Maybe he hated what was going on between you and Michael and was powerless to stop it.'

This was too much for Henrietta. 'Your father was a supreme egotist; it would never have occurred to him that anything was going on – which it wasn't.'

'My Father was a great man,' Leon shouted at her.

'No Leon.' She was shouting too. 'He was never great – brilliant – yes, and a perfectionist – but like most perfectionists he was utterly selfish.'

'I loved him Mother, he was my father – please don't run him down.'

They were standing facing each other six inches apart like two stags before a fight.

'And so did I Leon! I loved him with every fibre of my being. I lived my life through him; I had no other life. When he turned against me I couldn't cope...his death was a merciful release for both of us.'

'And for Michael too no doubt!'

'Michael brought me back to life.' She sighed wearily, broke away and stood looking out at the ocean. 'It's no good, is it? I should never have come. I'd hoped to convince you that my loving Michael in no way diminished the love I had for your father.'

Leon went and stood beside her. He put his arm round her shoulder. 'I'm very glad you came,' he said.

She slowly turned and looked up at him. Was he being sarcastic? He smiled sweetly back at her and asked if she would like to sit down. He pointed to a bench a few feet away on the walkway above the sand. She nodded gratefully. She felt emotionally drained, sapped dry. She had never been much good at anger; it did not suit her personality.

She had sat down on the bench but Leon remained standing with his back towards her.

'Aren't you going to sit?' she said.

'No, I prefer to stand. I have something extremely important to tell you.' He cleared his throat. 'We can't live in the past, Mother, we have to live in the present, it's all we have.'

'How true,' she said. And she had very little present left.

'I haven't finished,' he said, his back still turned. 'I want you to know that I have forgiven you.'

'Forgiven me but...?' She had not asked for his forgiveness just his understanding.

'The scars won't go away but I can live with them now. '

If this was the price she would have to pay to make peace with him again, so be it. Michael would have understood.

'Thank you Leon, that can't have been easy for you,' she said.

Leon turned round to face her. 'It wasn't. It's taken ten years of therapy to work my anger through.'

She sat looking up at him, her son; this man she no longer knew; the sadness of the situation overwhelmed her and she began to weep.

Leon looked concerned and sat down next to her. He took a handkerchief from his pocket and passed it to her. Henrietta dabbed her eyes and blew her nose.

'Sorry, darling,' she said, 'I've ruined your handkerchief.'

'What's a handkerchief between a mother and her son? You know it's good to cry, cleanses the soul, allows us to move forward. My analyst told me that.'

Henrietta nodded quietly trying to compose herself. She became aware that Leon was observing her intently; she felt his hand gently turning her head around to face him. She looked at him questioningly.

'You look very tired,' he said.

'I am. You're looking at me so strangely – what is it?'

'I don't wish to be unkind,' he said, running his fingers lightly over her face, 'but you don't look good.'

At last! Now they could talk. She had wondered when he would notice. She had had a facial and her hair re-styled, but then Leon was a doctor and they were trained to see beyond the outward appearance.

'It's my eyes isn't it, they're the giveaway? Arthur used to say they reflect the inner workings of the body.'

Leon agreed. 'Quite, but yours could be beautiful again.'

'Could be? What are you talking about?'

'I can make you look twenty years younger if you'd let me.'

Henrietta reeled back in horror. 'You want to make me look *younger*, is that what you are saying?'

Leon was no longer listening; he was on a mission. 'You've given in to age Mother, you've let it ravage your beauty, but I can change all that, it's not too late. I've been itching to get my hands on you since you arrived.'

'But what if I don't want to look *beautiful* again? Perhaps those things are no longer important to me.'

'Then they should be! If you look younger, you feel younger, if you feel younger you'll stop being tired of life. You'll be rejuvenated – please let me do it. Do it for *me* if you won't do it for yourself. Don't you think you owe me that?'

'Owe you!?' Henrietta's mouth dropped open in disbelief. 'Oh Leon, what an extraordinary request!'

He was smiling eagerly awaiting her answer. She was about to turn him down when the thought came into her head. 'I suppose, dear, I would have to have an anaesthetic?'

Leon laughed. 'Of course, you won't feel a thing, you'll be black and blue for a while but you'll convalesce with us and then we'll send you home a new woman.'

Henrietta smiled at him gratefully; who would have thought her son was going to be the answer to her unsaid prayers.

'Arthur used to tell me I looked like Ava Gardener, perhaps I could again.'

'That's right, he did. You've still got good bones. I'll see what we can do.'

Leon was in his element and could not stop smiling. He said it would be at least a week before they could proceed. There would be a lot of tests and x-rays and the structure all to be worked out on the computer. At this point Henrietta begged him not to furnish her with the details and said it would be good to spend some time with her grandchildren so they would remember her.

Leon had looked at her questioningly. 'Remember you?'

'As I am,' she said quickly 'the *real* me. After all I might die under the anaesthetic.'

'You won't die, Mother, you've got everything to live for.'

Henrietta watched the dawn breaking; the sky was a wonderful shade of pink – beautiful – heavenly even! She smiled to herself. Outside her room the hospital was stirring awake. She had better get into bed and finish the tape. She was first into theatre and they would shortly be coming to give her the pre-med she had requested. 'I want to be all woozy when you put me to sleep.' She picked up the tape machine for the last time.

*'So darling here I am. I hope you've been able to follow my rambling thoughts. I'm very comfortable here in my little cell – whoops! I mean room! Freudian slip! Though now I know what it must feel like waiting for the executioner. That was a joke Zoe, please don't read anything into that. No, I am **not** having second thoughts. I'm being treated like visiting royalty; Leon is using his finest team; he said that it wouldn't be ethical for him to operate himself. I didn't think I'd get away with it. I thought they'd find me out. I did tell them that I had had a heart attack,*

as I knew it would show up on my ECG. I also told them that I'd never had an anaesthetic; they had no reason to disbelieve me. The anaesthetist, a sweet little man, Chinese, warned me that there is a slight risk involved, particularly at my age. I felt rather deceitful. I even said to him if I pop off he must not be upset or blame himself; I remember how Michael used to feel when he lost a patient. "My bags are packed," I said, "I'm quite ready to go." I've told Leon that, several times, but he gets cross with me – thinks I'm questioning his ability. Please Zoe, do not blame Leon. If it hadn't been for him I would have found another way, probably Dignitas. You'll find all the papers in my desk at home. He has fulfilled my wishes. I have written him a long letter which I've entrusted to Melanie to give to him in the event of my death.'

The orange warning light flashed up on the tape recorder. Henrietta's stomach turned over.

'Oh dear! The tape is running out – we've no time left. You know how much I love you. Don't be sad Zoe, it's a beautiful exit: clean, painless, my mind still in tact. I've always loathed goodbyes, so au revoir my darling girl. Forgive me and thank you for loving me…'

The tape clicked off and then began to rewind at treble speed with Henrietta's voice distorted and high-pitched going backwards. She placed the machine on the bedside table and lay back exhausted on the pillows listening to her little life wiz by. She closed her eyes and hoped, when she finally awoke, it would be to face her Maker and not with the face of Ava Gardener.

4

Lightning Source UK Ltd.
Milton Keynes UK
UKOW030859170312

189129UK00001B/26/P

FEELING *the* FEAR
And other intriguing tales
CAROLYN PERTWEE

A young woman's life is turned upside down as she prepares
to confront her deepest fears. A group of friends is called
together to hear a clergyman's shocking revelation. A little
girl tries to make amends, in the only way she knows how.
A down-and-out variety performer remembers his dearest
companion. A tumultuous love affair is given an unusual new
perspective. A mother tries to mend a damaged relationship
with her son, but he's changed beyond recognition.

In these short stories from Carolyn Pertwee – tales of love,
betrayal, family turmoil, sexual misdemeanours, friendship,
sadness, pathos and even murder – a twist and a turn are
never far away.

Sometimes moving, frequently humorous, and always
supremely entertaining, these tales are guaranteed to keep
you intrigued.

Carolyn Pertwee

Alliance Publishing Press

ISBN 978-0-9552661-9-5

90000

9 780955 266195